# The Ground Upon Which I Stand

S. Stieglitz

# DEDICATION

This books is dedicated to my husband, without his tireless patience and relentless support, it may never have seen the light of day.

# CONTENTS

\* This story first appeared in *Tales of Gods and Monsters*. It has been edited for consistency and continuity purposes.

*"My actions are my only true belongings. I cannot escape the consequences of my actions. My actions are the ground upon which I stand."*

-Thích Nhất Hạnh

S. Stieglitz

# MYTHOS 101: INTRO TO THE OLD ONES*

# Mythos 101: Intro to the Old Ones

# Chapter One

Ramona woke to the sound of her alarm beeping; the tone piercing her skull like a jackhammer. She moaned irritably and slapped it off. It was early and she hadn't slept well; maybe that was why she was unusually sensitive to the alarm this morning. Peering over the edge of her bunk, she looked to see the alarm had woken her roommate. It didn't help her mood to see that Darla, her roommate, had let her boyfriend stay over. Again. Ramona had *no* idea what Darla saw in him. Well, besides being rich. He was nothing to look at and had the sneering manners of the entitled class.

Why he was at the same small, backwater college as her, she didn't know either. She would have assumed someone like him would have gone to an Ivy League school instead of a moss-covered institution like Derleth College.

Despite her feelings towards the entitled pig, Ramona got down off her bunk as quietly as possible. She liked Darla; there was no need to wake her up. She put on her clothes in the dark from behind the closet door. She didn't want to turn on the light and risk being seen, or worse, having to see either of them in any state of undress. Eww! She hoped whatever she put on wasn't too awful. Then again, it was an 8:00 am class; it was unlikely anyone else would be dressed any better.

She was almost to the door of her dorm room, backpack on her shoulder, shoes in hand, when her alarm went off again. *Dammit.* She must have only hit the snooze button. She scurried over to turn it off, but it was too late. The mound on the bed was moving.

Carlton rolled over and sat up. He didn't remember he was on the lower half of a bunk bed and caught his head on the underside of her mattress. She heard a surprised 'ouch' as the springs scraped his head.

"I say, if you *have* to wake me at this dreadful hour, *must* you do it more than once?" he asked peevishly.

Ramona knew she should apologize, but she was getting up for class, a perfectly good reason to have set the alarm. "It's off now," she muttered and started for the door again.

"Don't let it happen again," Carlton ordered. His tone, never pleasant, was especially grating today. It went straight under her skin like the sound of nails on a blackboard.

Ramona stopped dead, flipped on the light, and snarled, "What did you say?"

Carlton's mouth moved but no sounds came out. He sat blinking at the sudden light.

Ramona went on furiously, "This is *my* room, not yours. You don't have to be here." She paused briefly, surprised at herself. She wasn't shy or timid by nature, but she wasn't normally this hostile either. "What are you doing here anyway? Why aren't you in *your* room?"

Carlton glared at her as he pulled the blanket up to cover himself. Ramona glared back. As if she wanted to see his bony chest. "I was invited," Carlton arrogantly informed her.

*No duh*, Ramona thought to herself. She had assumed that much. "Doesn't Darla have class today?" she asked. "I think she has an 8:00 a.m. lecture today, too. She needs to be getting up now."

She stared at Carlton as she waited for him to wake Darla. Carlton, however, refused to say anything and laid back down on the bed.

*Jackass*, she swore in her head. Normally, she would have just left. Darla was old enough to make her own choices, and if she wanted to skip class, it was no business of hers. Today, however, was different. Today, awake for barely ten minutes, she could feel something was off; strange somehow. She had a sinking feeling in the pit of her stomach like she had forgotten to turn a paper in. No, more like dreading an upcoming exam that she hadn't studied for.

Ramona stood without moving as she struggled to identify what was going on. She told herself to calm down as she took a deep breath. *What was that smell?* Had they burned incense or something last night? Was that what she was reacting to? Irritated, she decided to make sure Darla wanted to skip class.

"Darla, hey roomie, time to get up," she called loudly.

No response.

Ramona didn't like getting near Carlton when he was completely clothed, much less now, but she set her jaw and went over to the bed. Fortunately, Darla was on the outside of the bed with Carlton near the wall. Ramona put a hand on Darla's shoulder and shook it gently. Still no response.

"Darla? C'mon, wake up." She put her hand on Darla's cheek; it was cool to the touch despite the blanket and her proximity to Carlton. Now that she was up close, she could see that Darla's lips were unusually pale. As she shook her more strongly, Darla moaned and slurred something incoherent. Concerned, she asked Carlton, "What were you two doing last night?"

"That is *none* of your business," Carlton sneered.

Taken aback, Ramona asked, "Aren't you worried about her?" Seeing that he wasn't, she went on, "Why aren't you worried? What is going on?" Her voice was getting louder as she got more anxious.

"Keep your voice down, you idiot," Carlton ordered.

Stung, like she had been hit, Ramona reacted without thinking. She stood up and screamed, "GET OUT OF MY ROOM NOW!"

Carlton recoiled in surprised; too stunned to say anything.

Ramona was done with him. She grabbed hold of the blanket and pulled fast and hard. Carlton watched as the blanket uncovered him, only clutching for it way too late.

"Get out! Out! Out! OUT!!" she screamed at him.

Carlton scrambled as he tried to obey, looking frantically for his pants. Picking them up from the floor, Ramona threw them into his face. He got out of bed, trying not to trip while putting the pants on at the same time. She threw his shirt towards him, then picked up his shoes and backpack. Turning her back on him, she opened the door to toss them into the hall, where they landed with loud thumps. Carlton ran past her, chasing after his stuff. He turned back, no doubt to say something insulting, but she was already slamming the door in his face.

## Chapter Two

After locking the door, Ramona leaned back against it, trying to catch her breath. She felt buzzed, like she had had too much caffeine. She couldn't believe she had caused such a scene. Darla wasn't going to be happy that she had treated her boyfriend so badly. *Dammit to hell.* What was going on with her today? She wanted to get to class, but now she couldn't leave Darla. Right or wrong, all the shouting should have woken her. The door vibrated as the RA knocked on it, saying, "Are you all right? Ramona? Darla?" More knocking. Apparently, she had woken someone up. Great.

Ramona unlocked and opened the door. Jill, the RA, was there, wearing a robe and her glasses. She was an upperclassman and nice enough. She wasn't sure how Jill would take getting screamed awake though.

"I'm okay," she told Jill.

Jill nodded and peered past her, looking around the room. "And Darla? Is she okay?"

Ramona hesitated; worried she would get Darla into trouble. Then she shook her head, as the concern to find out what was going on with Darla got the better of her. "She doesn't look too good to me," she told Jill, as she moved to open the door wider.

Jill gave her a puzzled look as she went in and over to Darla. She also shook her but then felt for a pulse. She pulled open one of Darla's eyes and even got in close to smell her breath. "This isn't good at all," she told Ramona. "I'm calling an ambulance." She pulled her phone from her robe pocket and started dialing.

Ramona was scared. She wasn't sure an ambulance was necessary, but even more scared that it might be.

After making the call, Jill told Ramona to stay with Darla as she left the dorm room. Ramona could hear her telling the other coeds to clear the hallway and to keep it clear. For a moment she stared around the room, numb with fear. Then, she snapped herself out of the haze. *I can handle this,* she told herself. She reminded herself that she was a nursing student and that she should be able to deal with a medical situation like this. Okay. What to do first? She went over and checked on Darla. Still breathing. She breathed a sigh of relief.

*Still breathing? Is that a nurse's assessment?* she reproached herself. She told herself to focus and took Darla's vitals. Breathing, shallow; pulse, weak; skin, cool but not clammy to the touch. What next? She assumed she would be asked what Darla had eaten or drank in the last twenty-four hours, or any medications she was taking, so she got up and looked around their room. There was nothing evident out on Darla's desk or dresser. They had a little refrigerator, but it only had water and soda in it. She rummaged through Darla's drawers, but other than racy underwear, she didn't find anything interesting.

She stopped looking as she heard the ambulance crew coming down the hallway. She got scared again and the room suddenly felt very stuffy. Taking a deep breath didn't help. In fact, she felt irritated again. Dammit, she was missing class!

Jill knocked perfunctorily on the door before opening it and coming in. She stood to one side and gestured for the EMTs to enter. Ramona moved to give the crew space to get to Darla.

They came in and went straight over to Darla. As they assessed her condition, they also asked Ramona for any details she could provide, as she expected they would.

Ramona told them what she could about what Darla may have eaten last, and that she didn't have any allergies or wasn't taking any medications that she knew of.

"I'm sorry; I know that isn't very helpful. She was on a date with Carlton last night. You should ask him; he could probably tell you more," she told the EMTs.

The older, male EMT immediately stopped what he was doing and looked up at her. "Carlton? Not Carlton Blayne?"

Ramona nodded, saying, "Yes. That's him. I think he's in the East dorms."

Only after the younger, female EMT nudged her partner, did he break eye contact with Ramona. She gave her partner a strange look before telling Ramona, "We'll ask him. Thank you for your help."

The older EMT cocked his head to one side and kind of shrugged one shoulder but didn't say anything. Ramona felt like he was saying, '*oh, no we won't*'.

The EMTs took Darla to the local hospital, strapped to a gurney; an oxygen mask covered her nose and mouth.

Jill had stayed close by while the EMTs worked. Once they left, she went over to Ramona and gave her arm a gentle squeeze, saying, "It's okay. They will take care of her, I'm sure." Peering into her eyes, Jill asked, "Are you okay?"

Ramona nodded, numbly. "I guess so." She didn't know what to say.

Leaving the room, Jill said, "I'm here if you want to talk, okay?"

Ramona just nodded again. She mechanically closed and locked the door. With Darla gone, the room felt weirdly empty. But it didn't smell anymore. She was glad of that.

## Mythos 101: Intro to the Old Ones

She sat down at her desk with a thump. It was still morning, but she didn't have any other classes to get to. She wondered what she should do. Study? That didn't feel right, somehow.

Now what?

# Chapter Three

Ramona sat, slumped in her desk chair, arms folded, as she went over what had just happened in her head. Her roommate had been taken to the hospital because she had had too much to drink or popped the wrong combination of pills, or something like that. Scary, sure, but not unheard of on a college campus.

As she thought about it, her fear left her. Darla was alive and being taken care of at the hospital. She was going to be fine. Ramona didn't allow for the possibility that she wasn't going to be fine.

What Ramona found herself feeling was anger. Not that weird irritation from earlier; just plain anger. She was angry at Darla for scaring her and she was also mad at her for what she did to herself. She knew better! And she was angry at Carlton. It was his fault. Darla hadn't been into heavy drinking or taking drugs before she started dating him. It had to be his fault.

He knew what had happened, whatever that was. He wasn't scared when Darla wasn't waking up, so he must have known why. He must know what she took or how much she drank. Or, he had given her something!

*And*, he hadn't wanted her to say anything. Darla could have been dying and Carlton didn't want her to make any noise! *That bastard!*

The more Ramona thought about it, the angrier she got at Carlton. She remembered the EMT's reaction at hearing his name. She had seen TV shows about families with 'old money' but this was her first experience with it.

She got up to walk furiously around the room. As the daughter of a single mother with no college education, she was used to living hand-to-mouth. She had dealt with snobs and entitled jerks all her life, but this was different. Carlton should be held responsible for his part in all this.

Ramona stopped pacing. Carlton *should* be held responsible.

As far as her academics went, the day was over. She took her class books out of her backpack and added a couple of bottles of water. After tossing in her phone charger, she slung it over her shoulder and left the room.

She walked quickly across the quad towards the dorms where the rich kids lived. Once there, she asked the first boy she saw where Carlton's room was. Not surprisingly, he knew. She stomped up the stairs and down the hall until she found his room. She knocked on his door lightly. Annoyed with herself for losing courage, having gone this far, she forced herself to knock harder.

There was movement inside. She listened at the door but didn't hear anything else. Banging on the door again, she called out, "Carlton? Are you in there? Open up!!"

The door opened, but not by Carlton. Surprised, Ramona gaped at the man. She had been prepared to lay into Carlton, but this wasn't him. She didn't know Carlton had a roommate. The man was young but somehow seemed older; handsome but not cute. A strange sense that something was off about him made her stomach tense, but she couldn't stop staring into his eyes.

The man smiled; he seemed amused at her reaction to him. Ramona continued to stare without saying anything. It was like the answer was right there; so close. What the question was, she had no idea.

Finally, the man broke eye contact by looking her up and down, before asking, "May I help you?"

His tone was strange, too, but again, she wasn't sure why. Something about it just didn't fit the face it was coming out of.

"I want to speak to Carlton," she told him mechanically. The strange feeling lessened as she pulled herself together, but it was still there.

"Yes, I gathered that. He is not in at the moment," he replied.

The man was calm and poised and wasn't sneering at her, but he was still amused.

Finding her courage, Ramona said, "I want to ask him what he gave Darla last night. Where is he?"

The man's smile vanished, though he continued to appear calm and poised. "And who is Darla to you that you are so incensed on her behalf?" he asked her.

Ramona felt her back stiffen in reaction to his insinuation. Taking it for granted that Carlton actually had slipped Darla something, she asked, "Who are you to Carlton? His roommate? His lawyer?" She didn't know why she asked him that; it made no sense. He looked young enough to be a college student but, at the same time, old enough to be a lawyer.

The man snorted at her; a sound that could have either been amusement or impatience.

"I am *not* Carlton's roommate and I have no time for lawyers…" he broke off suddenly. Ramona didn't know what he was going to say, but she was getting curious about him.

"So, what are you doing in his room?" she asked him.

"Impertinent. And immaterial," he replied. He eyed her up and down again. Seeing that she was less fascinated by him, he was no longer amused. "I will tell Mr. Blayne that you called for him, Miss…?"

"Guerrero. Thank you, Mister…?" Ramona asked, prompting him to give her his last name, at least.

"Curwen." He didn't smile and his face was stern, but his eyes glinted briefly as he spoke his name. Then, he stepped back inside and closed the door.

Wow. Now that he was gone, she felt let down somehow. It was like the time she faced down a bully at high school. At the time, she felt sure that they were going to get into a physical fight. At the last second, a teacher intervened and it all came to nothing. She was feeling that same sense of fear/anticipation/relief now as she did then.

She turned and walked down the hall and into the stairwell. She wanted to go where she could stop and get herself together without anyone seeing her.

*What is going on with me today?* she asked herself. First, she skipped class, then she screamed at Carlton, now she suddenly wanted to fight a strange man she just met. She gripped the utility pipe in the stairwell hard and leaned her head against the wall. The cool, painted concrete felt good against her forehead. She tried breathing deeply but stopped as all that air made her light-headed. Scared and unable to focus, she ran down the stairs and out of the dorm. She had to find Dex.

# Chapter Four

Dex would probably be in the science building. Dexter Phillips was a double major in Chemistry and Ancient History. He was also in his junior year, like her. And he was also her ex-boyfriend.

They dated all last year and it had been great. They met in the library and instantly hit it off. He found her choice of double majors as interesting and strange as she did his. She didn't see a connection between Chemistry and Ancient History, and he didn't see one between Nursing and Language Studies. They enjoyed studying together as much as hanging out in between. For a hard-core academic, he was surprisingly fun to be around. And he was good to her. He was the whole deal—smart, cute, and sweet; she had really fallen for him.

She broke up with him when she found out he was using his chemistry knowledge to make drugs. She also had reason to believe he too was using his product. It hurt like hell to break up with him, but she couldn't handle the drug use and everything that came with it. Even almost a year later, she still wished she could have been strong enough to deal with it. There were days when she still missed him, but she never called him.

Suddenly realizing that she was literally running to a guy she had broken up with, she stopped dead in the lobby of the chemistry building. Another student bumped into her, grumbled a terse 'Sorry,' and kept walking.

Dex wouldn't want to see her now. They hadn't spoken all year and it was close to the end of the spring term. Why would he help her after she had left him?

Standing in the lobby, with the other students walking in and out, around, and by her, she felt terrified and alone. She put her hands to her face and closed her eyes, overwhelmed by her emotions.

"Ramona? Ramona, are you all right?"

Ramona looked up and spun around at the voice. Dex's voice. Her chest heaved and her throat got tight as she fought the urge to throw herself into his arms.

"Whoa," he breathed faintly, taking an involuntary step back as he got a look and saw the state she was in. Then, he seemed to get a hold of himself.

"Are you okay?" he repeated, gently. "What happened?"

She shook her head but couldn't say anything. She was flipping out inside her head. As much as she had needed to see him a *second* ago, she felt ashamed and embarrassed at him seeing her like this. Now she just wanted to get *away* from him.

He could see she was about to run. Very calmly he said, "It's okay. Let's talk." He slowly came over to her. All she could do was meet his eyes.

His face turned grave as he got closer to her. He didn't take her in his arms, like she half-hoped, but instead took hold of her shirt at the shoulder and pulled it up as he leaned in close to sniff at it. Non-plussed she just stared at him, as he smelled her hair and then looked intently into her eyes.

"Come with me," he stated firmly, taking her hand.

She initially resisted, but then followed obediently as he led her through the chemistry building and down to one of the student laboratories.

She recognized the lab as his assigned workspace. He sat her down on the one stool and told her to wait. She watched him as he mixed water from the tap with a powder he took from a locked drawer. After stirring it, he held it out to her saying, "Drink this."

Without thinking, she took the glass and raised it to her lips.

*No. Wait,* she told herself. Looking up at him she said, "What the hell is this? And why should I drink it? It smells nasty, like something wet you dug up from your backyard."

Dex smiled even though his eyes were still concerned. "Ramona, it's okay. You've been drugged. What I am giving you will counteract the effects."

"Drugged? Me?" she asked incredulously.

"Want me to prove it to you?"

"Yeah. If you can."

"Drink it now," he ordered her sternly. His tone was hard and unyielding.

Ramona felt the glass at her lips before she realized what she was doing. She stopped again and stared at Dex.

He nodded. "You are reacting to the drug in your system. Well, partially. You seem to be fighting it."

She stared at the glass then back at Dex.

"I promise you, what I am giving you will help neutralize the effects a lot sooner than if you wait for your body to metabolize it on its own," Dex said reassuringly, as he gripped her other hand.

"Will it help neutralize my freaky mood swings?"

"I think so. I suspect they are a side effect from the drug or from you fighting it," he replied.

Desperate to get off the emotional roller coaster, she drank quickly, trying not to smell it as she did.

"Bleaaagh!" she gagged after downing the mixture. "That was awful! What was in that powder?"

Dex grinned at her reaction. "You probably don't want to know. You weren't too far off from your original guess."

Ramona couldn't tell if he was teasing her or not but decided to leave it for now.

"How did I get drugged? I didn't drink anything last night…" She broke off, suddenly realizing she couldn't remember much about the previous evening.

Dex backed away from her and leaned up against the wall. "It was probably someone close to you. Maybe like your boyfriend?"

Ramona didn't care for the question, but she could see that Dex was upset.

"I don't have a boyfriend," she replied honestly. "I haven't dated anyone since…last year."

Dex looked down briefly and shifted his feet before saying, "Okay, but it still had to be someone close to you. And I don't think it was in a drink. I could smell it on you."

"Smell? Like incense? Darla and her idiot boyfriend were together in our dorm room last night. I thought I smelled something this morning. Except, when I looked through Darla's stuff, I don't remember seeing an incense stick or anything like that."

"Do you normally go through your roommate's stuff?" he asked her.

"No! Darla had to be taken to the hospital and I was looking to see if she had pills or weed or anything. But, from what you are saying, it looks pretty certain that Carlton drugged Darla and I somehow got some, too."

"Carlton?" Dex said abruptly. "Not Carlton Blayne?"

"Yes, Carlton Blayne. He's a first-class jerk," Ramona said, exasperated that even Dex knew the name.

Dex looked at her like he was wondering if she was serious.

"What? He is a first-class jerk. I don't care how much money his family has."

"Ramona, what is the name of our college library?"

She thought for a second. It was a library. The brick-faced, four-story building on the west side of the quad. The best study cubes were on the 2nd floor. The library was called… the Blayne Library.

"Ohh."

"Yeah. His family doesn't just have money. They also have considerable *influence* over the people of this town and at this college. You really don't understand how much control they have here."

Ramona could see that Dex was completely serious but, really? Wasn't owning a town something that sheriffs did in old westerns? Or mobsters in New York or Boston?

Reacting to the look on her face, Dex went on. "Ramona, please. You don't know what you are close to right now."

Interrupting him, she said, "What? I'm in danger or something, you mean?"

"Yes. That is exactly what I mean."

# Chapter Five

Ramona laughed. She stopped when she saw the irritation in Dex's eyes. He wasn't kidding. "Danger? From Carlton? You really think that bony toothpick could hurt me?"

"That bony toothpick is the son of a High Priest of Cthulhu. He is the fourth generation of the Blayne family to be initiated into the worship of the Great Old One."

"Kha hu loo? Cat thu hoo?" Ramona said, attempting to mimic Dex.

Dex glared at her as he tried to determine if she was being serious or mocking. "Cthulhu," he repeated, pronouncing it slowly and enunciating the syllables.

"They are a real sect of worshippers, with very real power. You haven't heard of them because they don't want to be in the mainstream. They don't recruit followers; in fact, they are very selective as to who they initiate."

"So, where do Darla and I come in?" Ramona asking, deciding to hear him out. Darla had needed to be taken to the hospital and she had been drugged. Fact. And whatever Dex had given her was already starting to level her out.

"How long have Darla and Carlton been dating?" he asked her.

"I'm not sure. I think they were already a couple when we got back from winter break."

"And is she saying she is the One for him?"

Ramona nodded, rolling her eyes. "Oh yeah. I could hardly listen to her when she told me; it was all so school-girl and childish."

"I'm pretty sure you missed a lot of what she was telling you. But, do you believe it's real on either side?"

"On her side, I'd say she likes the presents and the prestige of being with a Blayne. On his, I don't believe he cares a rat's tail about her; he's just using her."

"For what?" pressed Dex.

"You mean besides sex?"

Dex nodded. "He can get that from any woman. Why do you think he's with Darla?"

She shrugged. "Her family is local. They don't live too far from Derleth. They do not have a lot of money. She's the only child. She is absolutely fanatical about the Blayne family." Ramona stopped as the pieces started to fit together. "She is what he wants, isn't she? She'll do anything he tells her to. Is that it?"

"A part of it, yes."

"But if that is true, why drug her? I mean, it would have to be something really out there for her not to agree with whatever Carlton says."

Dex's face was grave but his eyes were wary as he watched her think it through.

"You said High Priest and called them a sect like a religious order. Worshippers of a great God very few people even know about. Like a cult. Cultists can be fanatical. And ritualistic. Do they like their rituals?" she asked him, half amused at the thought of pagan rituals.

"Yes, that is one of the ways the followers derive power."

"Huh. What kind of rituals? Dancing naked in a circle? Sacrificing a chicken?" Ramona asked. She still thought all this was funny.

"No dancing. No chickens."

"Really? Then what...Wait. No. Sacrifice, as in, yes? Blood sacrifices, as in, human? As in Darla?!" Ramona jumped to her feet, almost shouting at Dex.

Dex didn't flinch and stayed leaning against the wall, eyes dark. He nodded slowly.

"*That bastard!*" she growled. "How did he think he was going to get away with it?"

"Because his family has, many times, for generations."

Ramona could only gape at him, speechless.

Finding her voice, she shook her head saying, "I cannot believe this town is that small. Really? The police, the families, they all just look the other way?"

"Yes. As I told you, don't underestimate their control over people here or their power to get what they want."

"Well, I'm glad Darla is at the hospital then, where he can't get to her."

As if on cue, Ramona's cell phone buzzed in her pocket. She took it out and not recognizing the number, answered tentatively, "Hello?"

Dex could only hear one side of the conversation.

"Yes, this is Ramona.

"Yes, I am Darla's roommate.

"Oh hello, Mrs. Owens.

"No, I don't know where Darla is. She isn't at the hospital?"

"Well, I haven't been back to our room since this morning, but I can go there now and call you back."

"No, it's okay. No bother. I hope everything is okay, too."

"Yes, I have your number. I'll go now. Bye for now."

Ramona looked at Dex, who stared back steadily.

"That was Darla's mother. Darla is gone from the hospital."

## Chapter Six

"We've got to do something. Carlton is going to hurt her. We've got to stop him!" Ramona was scared and angry, but at the same time, determined and eager to go and save Darla.

Putting his hands on her shoulders, Dex stared into her eyes and said, "No, we don't. You can't save her. In fact, it would be worse if you do."

*Huh?*

"What? Dex, are you serious? We can't save her? And we shouldn't even try? Worse how? Worse for who? Carlton? You?" Ramona sputtered, nearly incoherent. She couldn't believe what she was hearing from Dex of all people.

He replied, still calmly, "What's your plan? Call the police? They won't come; they know who pays their salaries and more importantly, the older cops know their guns would be useless."

"And don't ask about the state police. What are you going to say? My roommate is being sacrificed to a Great Old One, come quickly? They aren't going to believe you, and even if they did, you don't even know where they are."

"Dex, okay. Maybe the cops can't help, but there has to be something we can do. The knowledge, the power can't be all on one side!"

Dex's eyebrows arched in surprise. "Well, no. The power isn't all on one side. And there are ways to counter it. It's not easy; the timing is key." He sounded like a professor, logical and academic.

"Great! So, let's take the knowledge out of the classroom and into the field where we can do some good with it!" Ramona, excited, grabbed Dex's hand, ready to drag him out of the lab.

Dex shook his head. "No. You still don't get it. This isn't a simple showdown between Good and Evil. This is humans calling out across the void, awakening the Dreamer. When he comes it is on his terms; our laws and rules no longer apply."

"There is no 'winning,' no saving the day," Dex finished quietly.

Her eyes filled with tears at what she was hearing. Dex took her hands and squeezed gently.

Something in Ramona burned at the thought of doing nothing. She forgot all the crazy moods and weirdness of the morning. She pulled her hand free from Dex and put it on his cheek briefly, before suddenly slapping him hard.

"I will not stand by, watching, and doing nothing. I will fight against Carlton *and* his Gods."

Filled with righteous indignation, she shoved him with both hands. As he stumbled, she grabbed her backpack with one hand and yanked the door open with the other. It felt good to slam the door behind her, ignoring whatever it was Dex was trying to shout at her.

She was up the stairs and halfway across the quad before she suddenly realized she didn't know where she was going. She didn't know where Darla or Carlton were now, where they were going, or when the ritual or whatever was happening.

Dex might have had some idea. She didn't know how, but he sounded like he knew a lot about this Great Cthulhu.

So, what to do now?

It was late morning and she was starving. She hadn't eaten or drank anything other than that foul glass of water. She had gone through Darla's things in their room, so there was no need to go back there. Darla had a locker at the gymnasium; maybe she could find something there.

*Like crusty workout clothes?*

Annoyed with herself, Ramona decided to forget the gym and get some lunch. While eating, she thought of at least two places she should try—the library and Carlton's room. The library was always a good idea, as she could at least learn more about the history of the Blayne family. And if there were any clues to be found, they were definitely going to be in Carlton's room, as he was the main bad guy in all this.

After she ate, she went to the Blayne library, where not surprisingly, there were several books about the Blayne family and their history. Dex had been right about the family and their interest in Mysticism and the occult. The family didn't bother to hide it, their only discretion was not naming any specific deities.

One of the books had a drawing of the family's estate as it had been originally, before various pieces had either been sold or endowed to the college. Ramona picked up the book and took it to the front of the library where there was a large print of the college campus as it was today. She wanted to compare the two pictures of the Blayne estate.

After studying the two images she saw that, yes, there was a tract of land that had been part of the Blayne family estate but was now part of the college grounds. The area was largely wooded with some open spaces. The land was meant to provide the students with healthy hiking trails and the environment studies' students with a live laboratory to experiment in and many creatures to study.

It was a secluded area in the woods. It couldn't be that obvious, could it?

Unfortunately, it was a large enough area that would take a long time to canvass on foot. She decided to deal with that later. Maybe there would be something in Carlton's room.

## Chapter Seven

Ramona left the library through one of the back exits and skirted the college campus around its outer perimeter. She was trying not to be seen going to Carlton's dorm.

Once there, she studied the back of his dormitory. It was an older building and had a wrought iron fire escape. There was nothing to stand on, but after several tries, she managed to jump high enough to grab the stairs.

She hung from them as they stubbornly remained horizontal. As she wiggled and pulled, she could hear them creak, but they still didn't move. She let go and dropped to the ground, frustrated. She jumped up again, determined to yank them down. This time they moved, but not enough. Three attempts later, she was finally able to pull the stairs down.

She clambered up the stairs, trying to be quiet as the old iron creaked and groaned under her weight. The fire escape led directly to Carlton's window, of course. The Blayne family heir had to be protected.

Peering through the window, she didn't see anyone in the room. The window opened easily, and she carefully climbed in, after remembering to take off her backpack.

She immediately started rifling through his drawers and closet. All she discovered was that he wasn't a tidy person and didn't properly care for his very expensive wardrobe.

She moved on to his desk. Carlton's laptop was there, but locked. She swore to herself quietly. Opening his desk drawers, she found a small box containing a ring. Ugly, but obviously very expensive. She quickly put it back. The next drawer was the jackpot. It had Carlton's journal—leather-bound, highly ornate cover with heavy stiff paper. Ramona thought it was very nice. It was somewhat old school that Carlton kept a hand-written journal, but she needed as many clues as she could get.

From the dates, it looked like he had been writing in his journal since he was thirteen or fourteen. She skimmed through the beginning, not really wanting to read the thoughts of an adolescent boy.

She slowed down and started to read more carefully as it got closer to the present day and Carlton started making references to Darla. Huh. From what he wrote, it seemed as if he really cared about her. He talked about her being the One and how pleased his family was when he told them.

Was she wrong about Carlton? Here she was thinking that he was going sacrifice her and all he really was going to do was marry her! She felt like such an idiot. He had a ring and everything.

Ramona got up from the desk, ashamed of herself. She picked up her backpack and took one last look around the room. An old-style suitcase and leather satchel caught her eye. The suitcase contained a man's clothes, precisely folded and neatly packed, as well as a bag of toiletries. The satchel contained several books and a journal.

Ramona handled the journal carefully, almost in awe. It was old; maybe from the seventeen or eighteen century. The cover was plain leather with a strap that tied the book closed. The pages were thick and had a coarse texture. The pages were bound together using what looked like the oversewn technique. Pulling gently at the pages at the spine, she thought the book had been unbound and rebound at least once. Also, there were pages that were not as heavy as others; perhaps they were newer, more recently made.

Ramona thought it was a shame the owner had mixed in modern-day pages into such a piece of history. She forgot about Darla, fascinated by the old journal.

Flipping back to the beginning, she noted a name written on the inside front cover: J. Curwen. Suddenly remembering the man from this morning, she wondered if this could be his great-grandfather's journal.

Whoever this J. Curwen had been, he was definitely educated. He wrote in the ornate, cursive style commonly associated with the eighteenth century. Most of his journal was in English, though parts were in French. There was also a period of several months where he wrote solely in Italian.

From the date noted occasionally, he wrote sequentially for the most part, as one would expect, but the later pages seemed out of order. The type of ink varied from page to page, even between the front and back of the same page. Or if not the type or color of ink, the type of pen or type of nib differed. How very odd. Had the current Curwen rebound the book out of order? Why?

And what was being written varied as well. Sometimes it was the general long hand of a diary entry; in other places, it looked like he was writing down recipes or something. She couldn't tell without further study.

Suddenly she heard a noise from down the hall. Footsteps coming closer. When she heard keys jingle at a different door, she breathed a heavy sigh of relief. It wasn't Carlton; just someone else on this floor.

The near-miss reminded her she shouldn't be there, but she didn't want to leave the journal. She got out her phone and started taking pictures of the pages. The journal was old enough that the pages stayed open, allowing her to get fairly good images of the pages. She got into a rhythm; click, turn the page, click. It was tedious and tiring but she got the entire journal in just under an hour.

Ramona didn't appreciate how tired she was until the sound of keys startled her. *Damnit!* She hadn't heard him coming.

She stuffed her phone in her backpack and managed to get the journal back in the satchel and the satchel back next to the suitcase as she heard the key in the lock, then unlocking the door. She watched the door open as she frantically tried to decide if she should hide in the room or try to make it out the window.

Out of time, she was standing in the middle of the room when Carlton and Curwen opened the door and came in.

"What the...? What are you doing here?!" exclaimed Carlton.

# Chapter Eight

Scared but defiant, Ramona said nothing in return. Curwen closed the door and said, "It is of no matter! How fortuitous that you are, my dear. We've been wondering where you got to."

Ramona's heart was racing at getting caught. She breathed deeply, trying to calm herself down enough to explain.

She stammered, "I'm sorry. I know this is wrong. I was just worried about Darla." *'my dear?'* Who talks like that? Her brain was distracted and going off on its own. *Focus*, she told herself.

"Darla is fine, no thanks to you," growled Carlton.

Confused, Ramona started to protest, but Curwen, said, "Now, now, let's keep calm children, shall we?" He looked at Carlton sternly before continuing, "The young lady is just worried about her companion. No need to growl and frighten her off again."

Carlton glanced angrily from Curwen to Ramona and back again but said nothing.

Curwen frowning, told him, "The lady has apologized. A gentleman would respond."

Carlton scowled and tried to think of something to say.

Curwen stepped around Carlton to stand in front of Ramona. "Of course we accept your apology, Miss Guerrero.

We can only imagine how upset you must have been with your companion being so unwell."

"Thank you, Mr. Curwen. Yes, I was most upset," Ramona stammered politely. Her heart was still racing. She was reacting to both Carlton and Curwen, but in different ways. Despite finding out that he wanted to marry her, her instincts told her that Carlton was still a first-class weasel. And Curwen, he just felt *off* to her. His speech was weird, but standing near him again, her gut got tight and she tensed up, ready to run.

"Where is Darla, Mr. Curwen? I was told she left the hospital."

"She is downstairs, in our van. We just came up to collect a few things. Carlton and Miss Darla are on their way to get married, you see."

Pretending she hadn't found the ring, she said to Carlton, "What? Married? Uh. Congratulations. It's not even the end of term," she stumbled awkwardly.

"Uh. Well, no. Thank you. It's just the time was right now," Carlton replied, just as awkwardly.

"And so it is. Carlton has his best man," Curwen said, putting a hand to his chest, "And Miss Darla has her maid of honor, just like she wanted."

*What the flippin' hell?* Ramona's mind screeched to a panicked halt.

"It's a bit of shock, I'm sure. Miss Darla will explain it all. Come along now."

Ramona couldn't speak. She watched Curwen pick up his suitcase and satchel. Carlton took the ring from his desk and a garment bag from his closet. She didn't protest and followed between the two of them as they left the room and then the dorm.

In the parking lot, there was a large van with no windows. They led her around to the back and opened the door. She saw Darla sitting on the floor of the van, but no one else.

Glancing around, Ramona didn't see anyone else in the parking lot. Realizing it probably wouldn't make a difference if she did, she climbed into the van without a fight.

"Thank you, Miss Guerrero. I very much appreciate how reasonable you are behaving. We have a bit of a drive ahead of us, during which you and Miss Darla will have plenty of time to get yourselves ready for the ceremony," Curwen, ever so politely said, before abruptly closing the door of the van with a solid thump.

Ramona jumped as the door closed. It was too late now; there was no way out.

She felt the van start and drive off. She needed to get her mind back into the game. They couldn't be going to the nearby woods if they had plenty of time. Scared, she looked at Darla.

She couldn't see much in the darkness of the van. She felt around until she found the overhead lights and switched them on. She could now see Darla, who was looking at her calmly.

Darla was free; not bound or gagged. She didn't look like she had been harmed or even bruised in any way.

"Darla? Darla, are you okay?"

Darla nodded. "Yes, I'm fine. I'm getting married. Carlton and I are getting married," she replied mechanically.

Ramona didn't have to be a qualified nurse to know Darla was high as a kite. As drugged up as she was, Darla utterly believed she was marrying into the Blayne family. She was going to do whatever she was told, like an obedient little puppy.

Trapped and unsure where that left her, Ramona swore and cursed for a minute before calming down. She looked around the van to see what she could find. Disappointingly she didn't find tools or anything to use as a weapon. There were a couple of garment bags though.

Inside one of them, she found a simple, but well-made long white dress, as well as a beautiful, hand-sewn lace veil. Soft, slipper-like shoes were in the bottom of the bag.

The other bag had a long, red dress with intricate stitching around the bodice. There was no veil but there was a lovely, long finely made scarf. Somebody in the Blayne family had good taste.

"Time to get ready," Darla said, still in the unemotional, mechanical voice, as she started to unbutton her blouse.

Ramona sighed in resignation. Might as well play along until she could figure out what else to do.

A short time later, the van stopped. Ramona felt the engine turn off as the overhead light went out. She rolled up her clothes and crammed them into her backpack. The two girls sat together in the dark without speaking until the door of the van was opened by Curwen. Carlton was nearby. Both were dressed in robes; Curwen's was elaborate, whereas Carlton's was plain.

Ramona saw they were in the woods. It was late afternoon but there was still plenty of daylight. She got out of the van, wondering what was going to happen now. She assumed rituals took place in the dark of night, under a full moon or something.

She turned and helped Darla out of the van. Pretending to cooperate, she fussed over Darla, straightening her gown and making sure her veil fell just right. Carlton nodded at her smugly.

*Jackass,* Ramona silently cursed him.

She took a moment to see to herself; she smoothed her hair and made sure the scarf draped over her shoulders evenly. Curwen smiled charmingly at her altered appearance but frowned as he took note of her shoes. She had ignored the soft red slippers in her bag and was still wearing her running sneakers. She met his eyes and mutely dared him to argue.

He looked over at Carlton, who shrugged and walked away, not caring what she chose to wear on her feet.

Still frowning, though now at Carlton, Curwen hesitated before ultimately deciding to leave the issue of her footwear alone. He went over to Carlton and the two spoke quietly for a time.

Ramona could not hear everything Curwen said, but she caught the gist.

Curwen, '…as your advisor…attention to detail…not wise to leave her unbound…'

As for Carlton, she heard enough. "What is she going to do? It will be over for them both very soon."

# Chapter Nine

Carlton led the way through the woods, with Curwen bringing up the rear to make sure Ramona didn't make a break for it. The trail was level for a while and gradually inclined upward until they crested the hill. From the top, Ramona could see across the glen. Their college was several miles east. It wasn't that far away in a straight line; they must have had to go around the perimeter to get where they had parked.

She looked down and saw a couple dozen cultists, already in some sort of formation around a central point. They were chanting, but she couldn't recognize the language. The intensity of the chanting increased as they saw Carlton and Curwen.

Carlton again took the lead, down the hill and through the cultists. As they walked, Ramona couldn't believe what she was seeing, or rather who she was seeing. She recognized some fellow students, a couple of teachers, as well as several people from the town. There were just as many women as men. Great. Apparently, being a cultist was open to anyone.

Ramona stopped walking when she saw Dex. He was in a robe and chanting just like everyone else. At first, she felt sick, then as Curwen prodded her to keep moving, she got angry. Of course, he was one of them. How else could he have known so much?

He turned his head to follow her and closed his eyes briefly as she passed him but kept chanting. She felt betrayed, but at the same time, she knew he had tried to warn her.

Once at the center, she could see there was a stone slab. Carlton stood in front of the slab and began chanting. She still couldn't understand what he was saying but it sounded like the same language. As she listened, she could discern that what he was chanting was different from the others.

Without any warning, everything around her changed. The smell of air went from cool and earthy to hot, thick, and foul. She couldn't see anything past the chanting cultists; the college was gone and the light was different. It wasn't the light of a setting sun; it was darker, yet she could still see as clearly. What was the source of light? What was going on; were they in some sort of bubble?

She looked up and saw stars. They were moving. The ground beneath her feet was moving, rising and falling, like it was breathing; but at the same time, she wasn't moving. The stars suddenly stopped moving, now aligned in a pattern she did not recognize. She felt disorientated and slightly nauseous.

Only one thing was constant—the chanting of the cultists around her. They kept chanting the same thing, over and over again.

Darla stepped back into Ramona, afraid and shaking. Curwen, the only one other than herself who was not chanting, hissed, "Stand still, girl."

Darla immediately became still as a statue.

Carlton paused in his chanting and nodded to Curwen, who prodded the girls towards the slab. As she got close to him, Carlton took Darla's hand and put the ring on her finger. "Lie down, my bride," he ordered. Darla immediately obeyed, but her eyes were afraid.

Curwen gestured for Ramona to also lie down. When she hesitated, he suddenly pulled a long dagger from his robes and put the tip to her chest. She got on the slab, head to head with Darla.

Lying on the slab, she could *feel* the chanting of the cultists; a wave of sound hit her each time they repeated their litany.

Carlton resumed chanting, but it was different from what he was chanting before. She supposed they had moved into the next phase of the ritual. It certainly sounded like he was calling to something, or someone. Was Cthulhu considered a someone or a something?

He, too, repeated his chant, over and over. She started chanting with him. It helped center her against all the messed-up messages she was getting from her other senses—heat where there couldn't be any, light when it was getting dark, the earth breathing when it couldn't be.

The chanting made her feel invincible and drained at the same time. She was chanting so softly, it was doubtful anyone but Carlton and Darla could hear her. As she chanted, she started deliberately making mistakes. She didn't really know why, she simply wanted to do something completely different. She alternated her mistakes, misspeaking a phrase or speeding up the cadence; anything she could think of to throw Carlton off.

The look of loathing he gave her was actually pretty scary; so was the dagger he now had in his hand. He must have had one as well. Rather than look at him, she looked upwards at the stars.

That is when the sky opened its eye.

If she hadn't been chanting, she probably would have screamed in terror. Struck numb with fear, she went silent— the waves of chanting still crashing over her.

Distracted by her, Carlton missed the awakening. Curwen, standing next to him, raised Carlton's arm for him, and urgently told him, "Give the Great One your sacrifice!"

Ramona was transfixed by the eye which seemed to be focused on her. A tentacle pushed itself out of the sky and seemed to be reaching down for her.

*Oh hell no.*

"Darla, sit up and scream!" she shouted and writhed on the stone, trying to break free of her paralysis.

Darla sat up just as Carlton's blade was coming down towards her chest. Ramona rolled off the slab away from the men and landed with a hard thump. Darla was screaming and couldn't hear them ordering her to lie down.

Ramona got to her feet and grabbed Darla. She lost her footing as the earth moved under her and she fell, pulling Darla with her. Darla landed on top of her, still screaming.

From underneath her, Ramona shouted up in her ear, "Stop screaming now." Mercifully, Darla stopped.

That is when the other screams started.

# Chapter Ten

Ramona looked up and saw that the eye was angry. The tentacle that had been reaching for her thrashed about and slammed down hard, crushing a cultist.

Some cultists broke formation and ran away from the altar. She couldn't see where they went; they just disappeared into the blackness.

Two beasts erupted out of nowhere and started savaging anyone within their reach.

Darla, deathly pale, stared at the eye. The look on her face was eerily calm.

"No, don't look at it. Shut your eyes! Ramona ordered her.

"It can't get to you, I promise," she lied. She pulled Darla close against her, certain they were going to die.

"Ramona! Come here!" It was Dex. He was shouting to her. He was on his knees, digging or scratching something into the ground with a knife.

"Come with me," Ramona told Darla as she started dragging her towards Dex.

From behind them, they heard Carlton scream as the tentacle crashed down again. Looking back, she saw the remains of the crushed altar, wet with the blood of its last sacrifice.

She quickly looked at Darla; fortunately, her eyes were still closed. Good. "Come on. We have to get to Dex."

A cultist ran up and grabbed her arm, shouting, "This is all your fault!" He got her throat in his other hand and squeezed. She grabbed at his hand and pounded her fist on his arm. Behind him, she saw one of the beasts. It had just finished rending one of the cultists and now it looked their way. It started coming towards them. Ramona waited for the thud, expecting it to leap into them. Instead, the cultist seemed to erupt in fire. Screaming the man fell to the ground.

She didn't understand where the fire had come from, but at the moment she didn't care. Darla hadn't moved. She stood still amongst all the chaos, eyes still closed. "Let's keep moving," Ramona urgently told her.

They reached Dex, and now Ramona could see he had drawn some sort of symbol into the ground with his knife and he was standing at its center. "Step inside carefully," he ordered. "Don't break the lines."

"Step high," she ordered Darla, as they crossed into the symbol.

Dex started chanting.

More chanting? Really? What was this cult anyway?

As the beast breathed fire at them, Ramona ducked instinctively, pulling Darla down with her.

Nothing happened.

Looking up, she saw the fire, but it seemed to be hitting some kind of wall; they were safe.

Dex continued to chant. Changing her mind about chanting, she listened and tried to figure out the words, so she could join in.

Ramona saw that other cultists had the same idea as Dex, but they weren't as successful for some reason. The tentacle crashed to the ground and whipped through another cultist's protection like it was nothing.

Both the beasts joined together, and their combined force overpowered another one.

Curwen suddenly fell to the ground outside of their symbol. Looking up, Ramona saw a strange winged creature; from its shape, it should not have been able to fly. Curwen lay moaning on the ground. He was bleeding from a bite in his shoulder, but he still had hold of the dagger from before, which was wet with some gore.

Still chanting, Dex pulled a small bag from his robes and mimed reaching into the bag and making a flicking motion. He held the bag out to her.

Reaching over Darla, who hadn't moved, she took the bag. The flying creature landed on top of Curwen. Ramona, still inside the symbol, flicked the powder onto the creature.

It screeched in protest and slammed its head into the barrier, shaking it. Curwen taking advantage of the distraction, sliced at it with the dagger. It screeched again and swatted at him.

Taking a bigger pinch of dust, Ramona flicked again, this time at its face. As the burned creature writhed in pain, Curwen managed to get inside the symbol with them. Winded, obviously in pain from his fall, he still started chanting along with Dex.

The creature slammed its head into the barrier again, but it held. After several attempts, it gave up and left for more easy prey.

Both men looked at her and Dex gestured at her. They wanted her to help.

She closed her eyes to the carnage going on around her and concentrated on their chanting. She willed herself to only hear them. As she joined in, she felt that same surge of power as before, and like she was being drained. Desperately she wondered when it was going to stop.

# Chapter Eleven

Ramona woke up, flat on her back, on the cold, damp ground. Her head ached like she had a hangover. *Where am I,* she wondered. As she sat up, she heard someone making strange noises. Looking around she saw she was in the woods. To her left, there was a man dressed in robes, babbling incoherently.

For a brief moment, she could not recall anything, then her memories broke through and flooded her mind. The heat, the screams, but especially that Eye. She stood up, so unsteady she had to hold onto a nearby tree for support.

"Dex? Darla? Where are you?" she called out.

A shadow moved nearby. Afraid, she cringed as her heart started racing. The figure stopped moving.

"Ramona, it's me, Dex. Okay?"

She blinked trying to clear her vision and breathed to get herself under control. "Dex? I can't see you."

"It's a little dark under the trees at this time of night. I have a flashlight, but I didn't want to scare you even more. Sometimes the half-light can make a person look strange even when they aren't."

That was Dex. Same voice anyway. Just like a professor, logical and academic.

"It's okay, let me see you."

The light came on and Ramona saw what he meant. He didn't look like himself. His face looked gaunt in what light there was, and his shirt was streaked with something. Blood?

"Where are we? I mean, when? I mean, how did we get back?" she asked in a rush.

Dex walked slowly towards her. He handed her the flashlight, then tilted her face towards the light so he could get a good look at her eyes.

Apparently reassured, he answered, "It's the same night, Ramona. You passed out for a little while, but not long."

"But how did we get back? Where did we go? I have so many questions."

Dex shook his head. "Not now. I am relieved that you are okay, but there are more important matters that need to be seen to before I can answer you."

Angry, she said, "Like what? I've been through psychedelic hell."

Dex didn't say anything as he turned and walked away.

Ramona followed him. Her head was still aching, but her anger helped distract her from it. As she came out from under the trees and entered the clearing, she recognized what must have been the ritual site. It wasn't as dark without the cover of the trees and she could see more.

She walked around, looking for the bodies, but didn't see any. There were no bodies or part of bodies, and no blood. Fortunately, there were no fire beasts or strange flying creatures either.

The stone slab was there, and it was broken, but not crushed as she remembered. It looked more like some immense force had twisted it until it snapped.

"Where is everyone?" she asked nervously.

"They are dead, my dear. I would have thought you noticed," Curwen said, from behind her.

Jumping in fright, she turned quickly towards the voice, raising the flashlight like a weapon. Curwen, what was left of him, stood stolidly.

Hearing the implied accusation in his voice, Ramona said, "You think I killed them?"

"You do not see the causal effects of your actions, Miss Guerrero?" he asked her.

"I know I stopped Carlton from killing Darla. I stopped the ritual, yes."

"Naïve fool. You can't stop a ritual once it has begun. Carlton made an offer to the Dreamer and it was accepted. You interfered with his completing his agreement. What happened next was retaliation for reneging."

"No. I don't believe you," Ramona said defensively. She turned to Dex, looking for his support, but he shook his head again.

"I will answer you but not now. Mr. Curwen and I have certain matters to discuss."

Taken aback, Ramona made a rude face and continued walking around the site.

Dex turned to face Curwen. After making a formal bow he said, "Mr. Curwen, thank you for your assistance in maintaining the protection ward. It would not have held without you."

Curwen inclined his head. "Not at all. I could not have done it alone, Mr. Phillips."

"Yes, well, thank you for choosing me."

Curwen merely nodded and waited patiently, anticipating more to come.

Dex continued, "May I ask what you will be reporting to the Blayne family, sir?"

"The truth, Mr. Phillips. Young Mr. Blayne refused to follow the advice of his advisor. He failed to maintain his focus and lost control of the forces he was trying to summon.

He displeased the Great One, who then took what was owed to him."

"During the retaliation, I sought refuge with the one I deemed most capable. Together we weathered Cthulhu's displeasure, and then I assisted you with opening the portal to return us to our original location."

"Is this something we can agree on, Mr. Phillips? The family will be most upset at their loss, but I don't see any reason why we should bear any responsibility for it, nor should we be branded with shame for surviving."

Dex nodded agreement. "Yes, certainly, Mr. Curwen. You have my full support."

Curwen waited until Dex continued.

"What about the others? What happens now? Only five of us survived, not counting the sacrifices. The minds of the other three are still with the Dreamer, even though their bodies are here. Who will inform the families of those who did not return?"

Those were not the questions Curwen was expecting. "As advisor, it is my responsibility to inform the High Priest, who will no doubt delegate all such tasks to me. It will be unpleasant, but I should do what I can to assist during this time of grief. This will include arranging for the transport of the three to the facility outside of Arkham, as well as the more tedious tasks of cleansing the site, removing now unowned vehicles, and such."

"You are injured and must be exhausted from the effort to maintain the protection ward, Mr. Curwen."

"No less than you, I'm sure. And the portal required a great deal of your blood. I am amazed at your fortitude and equally impressed at how well-prepared you were."

Curwen watched Dex tense up. Eyeing Dex closely, he said, "As if you were expecting things to go wrong."

Dex ground his teeth but decided to come clean. "I thought it was possible, yes. I would have done anything to keep her from being part of the ritual, but she refused my help. Once there, I did nothing to adversely impact the ritual."

"I knew many of those men and women personally; I grew up with some of them. I did *not* cause their deaths, Mr. Curwen." He stopped speaking and waited for Curwen to nod, to at least tacitly agree that he had not adversely impacted the ritual. Once he did, Dex went on.

"I know Ramona and I know how strong she is. Yes, I thought it possible she could cause problems and I prepared for the worst. Does my telling you this change your report to Mr. Blayne?"

Curwen considered his answer for a moment. "I would have preferred to have been informed of Ms. Guerrero's potential, but as you are being candid, so shall I. I, too, saw her strength and I bear some responsibility for underestimating her. Therefore, no, I will not change my report to Mr. Blayne, but should he ask for details, I will give them to him."

"Yes, about that," Dex began, his tone more businesslike. "As advisor, you have the heavy responsibility of a failed ritual and the many unpleasant tasks that come along with it. And you are both exhausted and grievously injured. Your wound is very hard to treat and, if I am not mistaken, already beginning to fester."

"Given his grief, I am doubtful Mr. Blayne will allow you the time or lend you the resources to treat it properly. You will soon be in severe discomfort."

"Do you have an alternative, perhaps a proposal, Mr. Phillips?" Curwen sounded intrigued.

"Yes, Mr. Curwen. I offer my assistance with fulfilling your responsibilities, including the care and transport of *the* sacrifice to a medical facility. Darla is not well, but perhaps not so far gone as to be untreatable."

"In turn, you will say nothing about a second sacrifice. Ramona was never there. You would report the details of how or why Carlton lost control with fewer specifics." Dex paused as he attempted to gauge Curwen's interest.

Seeing that Curwen was listening, Dex went on. "I understand this could be difficult, especially given your current condition. I could be of some use there, as well. I have access to certain components that would help in treating your wound and alleviating much of the discomfort."

"I see. I find your offer very tempting," Curwen replied. "However, forgetting a lady as unique as Ms. Guerrero will be difficult. Her actions influenced Miss Darla, as well. There would be a great deal of effort involved in keeping her out of any narrative, Mr. Phillips."

Dex wasn't ready to give up. "I said I knew many of the men and women here tonight personally. I know who will be missed and who will not. And only you and I know who made it back. Perhaps only two others came back, in addition to ourselves."

"What are you suggesting exactly?"

"Fred Bowen—the man currently catatonic and huddled by the large pine tree to your left. His body is completely uninjured and would be a significant improvement over the body you are currently in."

Curwen snorted in amusement. "You surprise me. You have much more depth than I was given to understand."

"Yes, I would like to agree, however, I regret in my current condition I could not perform the transfer ritual by myself. I would need assistance. Are you willing to perform the ritual with me?"

"Yes. Do we have an agreement, Mr. Curwen?" said Dex, offering his hand.

"Yes, Mr. Phillips, we do," replied Curwen, as he took Dex's hand and shook it firmly.

# Chapter Twelve

Ramona sat down heavily on the bench outside of her dorm; the events of the last three weeks going through her head. It had been very difficult, and she was exhausted in every way a person could be mentally, physically, and spiritually; she was drained.

The night after the ritual hadn't been too bad. Looking back now, she realized what happened in the woods hadn't really sunk in yet.

After the two men talked, Dex took her and Darla away from the ritual site using one of the cultists' cars. He drove Darla to the hospital and had her admitted, telling the hospital staff that she was suffering the effects of a bad acid trip and to treat her accordingly.

Ramona waited in the car, sullen, indignant, sore, exhausted, dirty, and just plain mad at Dex. She wanted him to take care of her and he was doing everything but helping her. *Jerk.*

He dropped her off at her dorm, promising again that they would talk later. She was past livid when the last thing he did was to take the scarf from her shoulders as she got out. It was a nice scarf; she had wanted to keep it as a memento.

She got up to her room, showered, and passed out in her bed for the rest of the night in a deep, dreamless sleep.

She waited all weekend for something to happen, but it didn't; nothing did. No news reports of strange beasts running around town, no reports of weird eyes in the sky, and not even a mention of anyone missing.

Ramona thought Darla's mother would call with an update on Darla, but she didn't too. Dex had adamantly told her, repeatedly, not to call the Owens or even make any reference to the ritual to *anyone*. Yeah, whatever. Like anyone would believe her. She would sound delusional, and she didn't want to get herself taken to some loony bin. He should give her some credit.

It all started to sink in on Monday when she went to her classes. There were empty desks, but no one said *anything*. It was freaky how everyone seemed to know not to ask any questions.

Anyway, the first week after the ritual passed all right—academically speaking. It was the last week of classes for the year. She focused on just getting through the last few classes and nothing else. She ignored how empty their dorm room was without Darla. She told herself that her roomie would be back any day now.

The second week was harder because she had her final exams. She wanted to believe that it was the stress of the exams that caused her to dream about the eye and how angry it looked. Ramona was sure that she would start sleeping again once the finals were over.

The third week was the worst. It was when everything fell apart. It was the time of year when most students partied, but not her.

First, she was called to the administrator's office to be informed that her scholarship had been cancelled. As she didn't have any money or alternate financing, that meant her college career was over.

Mrs. Owen finally contacted her, but it wasn't with the good news she was expecting. Darla had been discharged from the hospital but was still suffering the effects of the 'acid trip.' Romana could hear the quotes over the phone.

Hearing about Darla's nightmares made Ramona more uncomfortable about her own bad dreams; the call got worse. Mrs. Owen refused to let Ramona come and see Darla, saying it wasn't a good time, as on top of her health issues, she was also mourning the loss of her beloved fiancée.

Ramona asked if they wanted her to talk to the school administrators on Darla's behalf about making up her final exams but Mrs. Owen said it wasn't necessary. Darla would not be coming back to Derleth. In fact, the entire family was leaving the area. Apparently, Mr. Owen had lost his job.

Ramona didn't know why that meant the family had to leave town but she didn't think she should pry. Finally, Mrs. Owen asked Ramona to pack up Darla's belongings and to work with Jill on getting them sent home. Apparently, the one bright spot was that the Blayne family was covering Darla's medical costs as well as some of the family's expenses to leave the town.

Ramona promised she would. Mrs. Owen thanked her and abruptly ended the call before Ramona could say anything else. She didn't get a chance to say goodbye to Darla.

Lonely and sad, she packed up Darla's things, still sure she had done the right thing when she saved her from being sacrificed by Carlton.

The final straw came when she got a call from the folks she had arranged to work for over the summer. They told her they no longer needed her services.

She had arranged to work as an assistant caregiver for a family in the next town. It had been perfect. She was getting experience in her field, getting paid, and best of all, it was a live-in position; she wouldn't have had any living expenses.

After ending the call, she sank down onto the floor and cried. She cried for a long time before getting up to throw a tantrum. She shouted, she threw things, she kicked furniture. It wasn't fair! She had done the right thing!

Spent, she sank down to the floor again and put her head in her arms. She heard the sound of the cultists screaming in her head. Was Curwen right? Was it her fault all those people died?

She jumped at the sound of knocking. It was Jill. She was telling her it was time for her to leave the dorm. After helping her bring her boxes outside, Jill hugged her and told her to have a good summer. Ramona hadn't told anyone she wasn't coming back. As she left, Ramona sat down heavily on the bench outside of the dorm, spent and scared.

*What now?*

# Chapter Thirteen

Ramona wasn't sure how long she sat in her funk before Dex was suddenly in front of her. She watched as he sat himself down beside her. "Hey," was all he said.

Glancing over at him, she was surprised at his appearance. He looked like he had lost weight, especially in his face. His left forearm was wrapped in gauze.

"You look terrible!"

Making a wry face, he said, "Thanks. You aren't looking all that great yourself."

"I'm sorry; I meant, are you okay? What happened?" She went on hurriedly, seeing the incredulous look. "Not *that*, I mean your arm; I don't remember your arm being injured."

"Maybe we should start with what you do remember then."

"Well, I don't remember the night before the ritual. I remember all of Friday definitely up to the part where Darla and I were made to lie down on the cold stone."

"And then?" Dex prompted her gently.

"There was a *lot* of chanting. I couldn't tell which language, which is strange because that is my thing. What language was the chanting in?"

He reached over and gently squeezed her hand. "It's normal to deflect. If you don't want to talk about it, I understand. If you do, please focus. What happened next?"

Taking a deep breath, she continued, "Things got all warp-y and weird. It was almost as if we weren't still in the woods."

"I started chanting, too, along with Carlton, but I deliberately tried to mess him up."

Dex's eyebrows went up in surprise. "Really? I didn't hear that. I knew he was distracted but I didn't know by what, or rather whom. Go on."

"Well, I knew Darla was in a suggestive state because of the drugs. I think whatever she had been given was wearing off, too, because she was scared. She didn't want to be sacrificed."

Ramona paused before continuing quietly, "I told her to sit up and to start screaming."

"I didn't know what would happen, I swear!" she finished in a rush, her voice high.

Dex reached for her hand again but didn't say anything.

"Then, there were screams and beasts and eyes in the sky…no, the eye was first. You called us over. Curwen dropped from the sky. More chanting, powder flicks, more chanting, and then, I woke up on the ground somewhere in the woods, feeling hungover."

"I couldn't believe you would rather talk with Curwen than take care of me, but eventually you took us away." Ramona stopped there, wanting him to say something.

Dex took a deep breath and let it out. He let go of her hand to lean forward over his knees, thinking.

"Did I miss anything?" she asked him. "Look, I'm sorry about those cultists, but I really didn't know there would be weird dogs and weirder flying things."

"Those cultists were people; women and men like you and me. I knew them; a lot of them were my friends!" Dex burst out, angry. "Yes, I know you didn't know what you were doing, but the least you could do is give those *people* who died some respect."

Ramona looked down as her eyes filled with tears. She cleared her throat to loosen it. "Yes, you are right. I'm sorry. I am so very sorry."

Dex saw she was crying but looked away for a moment until deciding to put his arm out behind her. She gratefully leaned against him still crying. Eventually, she sat up, wiping at her eyes.

Dex also sat back and in a voice that was rough with emotion, said, "Yes, you did miss a few things, but let's start with why I treated you like I did."

"I had no idea what state you were in mentally, after seeing what you did for the first time. Not everyone can handle the 'weirdness', you know. I was relieved you weren't insane. And afterwards, no, I wasn't going to treat you like a child and say 'there, there.' You needed to hold yourself together; I couldn't do that for you. And think triage, Nurse Guerrero; you weren't the worst hurt person there."

Ramona hung her head again, this time in shame. "I'm sorry."

She suddenly shifted moods and asked angrily, "Why didn't you tell me? How am I supposed to have known? I couldn't know what I didn't know! Why didn't you tell me?"

"Tell you what, exactly?" he asked her, still angry. "You ran from me, us, when you found out I used drugs every once in a while. You're saying you could have handled the worship of non-Judeo-Christian Gods?"

She shifted nervously on the bench, "Maybe not then, but I want to know now. I want to know if you are willing to tell me."

"Why? The best thing for you is to get away from here and forget everything you saw and go back to taking care of yourself," Dex said bitterly. She had had no idea how much their breakup had hurt him.

She sat straight up, indignant, "Now, you, get something straight. It wasn't every once in a while, it wasn't just a little weed, and it was getting worse. You didn't listen to anything I said back then. The final straw was when some of my pain pills went missing."

It was Dex's turn to hang his head.

"I know what I caused to happen was horrible, but was it wrong? Was saving Darla wrong? What is this God who demands sacrifices? Why worship him if there are such consequences? What happened to your arm and why do you look like hell three weeks after it was over?"

He looked at her for a time, trying to decide how to answer.

Finally, he said, "I suppose it could be argued that it wasn't *wrong*, especially if she didn't want to be sacrificed. There are those who would argue that it *was* her choice or even that it was her duty to serve. Looking at it as an outsider like yourself, from a moral standpoint, I can agree that it wasn't wrong to disrupt the ritual, especially as you were being sacrificed, too."

Dex continued speaking without looking at her. "Cthulhu is an Elder God, from beyond the void. He demands nothing; it is us, we are the ones who ask of him. Many worship him for the power that he can grant so much so that they are willing to take the risks and suffer the consequences," Dex was speaking as an academic again. She was hearing what he was saying, and at the same time, realizing how much she had missed him this past year.

"Dex, you say 'us' in some places, like you believe, but then you say 'they' like it isn't you. Which is it? What do you believe?"

"Ramona, I believe. Cthulhu is real, the benefits are real."

"I was born into a family who has a history of worship, yet I am not sure of my place. I am a practitioner with extensive knowledge, but I don't crave power like some."

"A practitioner? What does that mean?" she asked.

"Any neophyte can participate. Learning the litany isn't hard. I have participated in many rituals since I came of age." He paused to see if she understood.

"You saw people sacrificed when you were young?"

He nodded. "I was told it was our way. Knowledge, power, sacrifice, ritual is all bound together; you cannot have anyone part without the others. And as you found out, disrupting a ritual isn't really an option, even if you can."

She took his hand. "Go on."

"A practitioner can create, or cast if you will, like a spell in a way. What you saw me do was create a protected area using the symbol to give it a form, a shape, and my will to make the walls. You and Curwen helped me; you both gave of your will and your energy made the barrier stronger."

"And your arm?"

"We *did* leave the woods. Had the ritual been successfully completed, Carlton would have ensured we returned safely. I had to open a portal to get us back here. My will alone was not enough. I needed to give my blood to make it work."

"I had no idea, Dex," Ramona breathed. "Will you be okay? Why do you look like it just happened?"

Relieved that she didn't ask about *where* they had gone, Dex quickly reassured her that he would be fine.

"I'm glad you will be okay, Dex, but I don't think you are telling me everything. What were you and Curwen talking about?"

Dex ground his teeth. "You. He and I needed to come to an understanding about what he would say about you."

Ramona knew better than doubt him at this point. "Why?"

"The Blayne family is strong and powerful; they would have destroyed you for causing the death of their son."

Ramona shuddered at his choice of words. "What did you have to do to protect me?"

"Curwen was hurt and needed more care than any regular medical doctor could have provided. I agreed to help him if he 'forgot' all about you."

"Just more will? More blood?"

He shook his head. "Not just that. A sacrifice was required."

"Dex! You had to kill someone for me?"

"In this case, it was a mercy killing. Like I said before, not everyone can handle seeing Cthulhu. And to be honest, it wasn't my first."

Ramona tried to not let that piece of honesty sink in. "But, are you saying that Darla isn't going to be okay, ever?"

"Darla has a chance. She has been through a lot, but it's possible she will find a way to cope."

Ramona prayed silently, hoping she would okay.

"Dex, I don't know what to say. You saved me after I got your friends killed. I don't know what to do or say to thank you. And I still don't understand. I believe you, I think. The alternative would be that I was also on some sort of acid trip."

"Maybe that would be better. Maybe I should just forget everything and start over somewhere else. It's not like I can stay here," she finished bitterly.

She waited until he asked, "What happened?"

"They took my scholarship! And my summer job! Can they do that?"

"The Blayne family, you mean?" Dex considered the question for a moment, "Well, yes, but I don't think it was them. They wouldn't be that obvious. I doubt it was anyone's deliberate action, probably just the negative effects of the failed ritual. Think bad karmic blowback."

"Is that what happened to Darla? Is that why her father lost his job?"

"That I think was the Blayne's doing. They knew Darla was Carlton's intended sacrifice. She is alive, he is dead; they know something went wrong. They don't know what, but they don't want the Owens around anymore," explained Dex.

"So why pay Darla's medical expenses?"

"Think in terms of a lord or baron taking care of his serfs. They rule, the serfs obey. The lord of the manor provides, and the serfs give their loyalty."

Ramona was shocked, "In America? Here? But so many people; that would mean that everyone is involved."

Dex nodded. "The entire town? Yes, they are. Can you think of anywhere else where I could drop off a young woman in a torn dress, tell them to treat her for a bad acid trip, and walk out without any questions?"

"The people choose to do it because they believe and because, for the most part, they get a free ride. They just hope they or someone from their family isn't called upon to be at the center of the ritual."

Ramona was skeptical. "The Owens had Darla, knowing that one day she might be taken from them? They must have known what Carlton wanted when he dated her. And they were okay with this? Mrs. Owen, too? No way."

"Yes. She at least knew and didn't stop it, though she might have had some doubts. Sometimes both parents agree, sometimes it's just one, but the other goes along with it. Believe me, the Owens benefited from Carlton choosing Darla."

"When the ritual wasn't completed, the Blayne family felt the covenant between them was broken and dismissed the Owens. In their position, they didn't want to appear petty or spiteful, so they graciously paid for Darla's medical expenses, while showing Mr. Owen the door."

"Damn! That's cold," exclaimed Romana.

Dex nodded. "Yes, in a way, but it is a choice. No one has to stay; they are free to leave at any time." He looked at her meaningfully.

She slumped back against the bench and tried to think. Dex leaned back, got himself comfortable, and waited patiently. As she worked through it, she spoke in disjointed sentences, not looking at him:

"I'm sorry I hurt you when we broke up."

"Thank you for saving my life…at least twice."

"I'm sorry I killed your friends."

"I hope you can forgive me one day."

"I missed you every day we weren't together."

"I wish there was some way we could work it all out."

Dex turned his head to look at her and just said, "Me, too."

Ramona quickly looked at him, wondering if he meant 'me too' as in he missed her, or that he hoped he could forgive her, or did he want to work things out between them?

Watching her, he smiled and said, "Yes."

Half-frustrated, half-elated, she moved over and put her arms around him, her head on his shoulder. He put his arms around her, holding her against him.

"I want to know more about who you are," she whispered.

"Good luck with that, I'm still trying to figure it out myself."

"I mean it."

"Ramona, there is a lot you don't know about me and my family. Big stuff."

"Do you intend to sacrifice me to your Great Elder God?"

"No. If I did, I would have done it last year, before we broke up."

Ramona's head snapped up to look him in his eyes. "You are kidding, right?"

"Yes," he said, while shaking his head no.

## Mythos 101: Intro to the Old Ones

"Want to come and stay with me at my family's house over the summer? We would have time to talk and I could teach you about Cthulhu, if you want. What do you say?"

She smiled, "Sure, sounds like a great idea."

# HOMECOMING

# Homecoming

# Chapter One

Ramona sat in the passenger side of Dexter's van, eyes closed, head back against the seat, as he drove them who-knew-where.

The past several weeks had been hard on her, starting with participating in her first ritual to the Great Old One.

On the downside, she had been one of the sacrifices. On the upside, she had managed to stop the ritual before she and the other sacrifice were slaughtered.

Unfortunately, the consequences of not completing the ritual had been catastrophic. Cthulhu's displeasure had resulted in the death of almost everyone at the ritual. Ramona wasn't sure how many had actually survived, but she knew that of the few that did, several of them had been taken directly to a mental institution outside of Arkham.

Her college roommate, the other sacrifice, had been taken to a medical hospital. The last Ramona had been told was that it was still undetermined whether or not she would recover; apparently, she was suffering from severe nightmares.

Dexter, or just Dex, as she called him, had saved her from Cthulhu's wrath after she had disrupted the ritual. He was her ex-boyfriend. She only recently found out he was a practitioner of the mythos.

Ramona wasn't sure if practitioner was the right term for Dex. It was what he had called himself, but it didn't sound right to her; cultist wasn't right either. She was still too new to it all to understand the 'religion' around the worship of one, who was, from what Dex said, an Elder God from beyond the void.

It almost unbelievable, but she had seen it for herself.

After the ritual, her life didn't go back to normal. Due to some sort of disrupted ritual 'blowback', she lost her scholarship for the next year. For her this meant her college days were over. She also lost her summer job, which was a double hit because it had been a live-in position. She was out of job as well as a place to live.

Dex had saved her, again, this time by inviting her to stay with him at his parent's house for the summer. It was the end of their academic year, so the van was packed with their stuff from their dorm rooms.

Ramona knew she should probably run as fast and as far as she could away from Dex and his Elder Dreamer God, but she didn't want to. What happened at the ritual still haunted her. She was indirectly responsible for the deaths of many people, and even if it was arguably in self-defense, she could still hear their screams in her dreams.

If she ran now, she would be running forever. Worse; something deep in her gut was terrified that whatever was in her dreams would eventually catch her. If she couldn't run, she would have to face it. In her mind, that meant learning all she could about Cthulhu and the mythos.

It wasn't just that though; she was curious about the 'religion', if that is what it was, that was so powerful, yet so few seemed to know about it. She was curious about everything; their rituals, their practices, and even the language of their chants. The study of languages had been one of her majors.

Then, there was Dex. She had broken up with him the previous year and had regretted it every day since. Despite everything, he had saved her on the night of the ritual. And after that, he had made some sort of deal or something that had protected her from the wrath of the family of the Priest that had been killed.

Ramona was still unsure of the details, but apparently, it had involved a sacrifice on his part, or something like that.

She also wasn't sure where this left them as a couple. He had saved her life twice over, despite the fact that she had gotten a lot of his friends killed *and* almost got him killed, too.

After everything, he had asked her if she wanted to come and stay with him at his parent's place over the summer and learn about the mythos.

She looked over at Dex, who was driving in silence; no radio.

Seeing her look at him, he asked, "What?"

"Nothing. Just thinking."

Changing her mind suddenly, she continued quickly, "Okay, tell me: Why are you being so nice to me after everything that happened?" she asked.

Dex smiled briefly before saying, "Ramona, I am *not* going to sacrifice you. Really. Yes, I am still upset about what happened but not like that."

She paused briefly before deciding to risk asking him directly, "Are you saying you want us to get back together, even after everything that happened?"

He looked at her for a long moment, before dragging his eyes back to the road. Finally, he said, "Yes. If you want to, I'd like us to get back together."

"Oh. Well, I've missed you and, yes, I would like to be with you again, but what about the drugs and the dealing?" His drug use was why she had broken up with him.

"I'm clean; I swear. I didn't like losing you, and after you left, I decided I had to do something about it." He sounded sincere.

"Does your Group have rehabs and stuff?" she asked him.

He gave her a hard look. "Yes. The people in this area are very well-educated and highly skilled in their professions. They believe in medicine and science, just like a lot of other people. They just choose not to worship Judeo-Christian Gods."

"What about the dealing?" she pressed him.

"I never dealt. You got that part wrong. I wasn't cooking anything in my study lab. I was studying and practicing incantations."

Ramona believed him about getting clean and about not dealing, but she was still unsure about why he would want to be with someone who nearly got him killed.

Dex knew she was uncertain and said gently, "It's okay. I'm not trying to rush you. I said we would talk, and we will. There is a lot I want to tell you, if you still want to hear it."

She reached out and he took his hand off the steering wheel to take her hand. Holding his hand tightly, she said softly, "Yes, I do."

# Chapter Two

Having agreed to talk, they both fell silent. Ramona hadn't asked where exactly they were going, but at the moment she didn't care. She was more relaxed now than she had been in weeks.

Dex eventually pulled off the road to gas up and get them both something to drink. As they headed back to the van, she suddenly stopped.

"You okay?" Dex asked her.

"Where did you get the van? I don't remember you driving a van."

Dex continued walking as he said, "Her folks said I could keep it. They didn't have a need for it anymore."

'*Her*?' Her who? Ramona was instantly jealous. She got into the van without saying anything, but she closed the door harder than she intended.

Dex got in and just looked at her, almost daring her to ask. She turned her head away and looked out the window.

He looked away, started the van, and got back out on the road.

"I think this is the van Carlton Blayne used to take Darla and me to the woods for the ritual."

"He's dead and you were never there," he answered curtly.

Ramona was assailed by conflicting emotions. She was still jealous but whoever 'she' was, 'she' was probably dead.

## Homecoming

Ramona also didn't like essentially being told not to talk about that night, but at the same time, she understood it was for her own protection. No one could know she had been there and survived. She felt guilty for using a dead woman's van to transport her stuff to Dex's parents.

She wanted to ask Dex if he had brought 'her' home to meet his parents. She wanted to know how serious they had been, and was either of them the other's Chosen One? Like Darla had been Carlton's Chosen One—his sacrifice to Cthulhu. Had it been like that?

"When I said I would tell you everything, I didn't mean *everything*, you know," Dex told her. He had been watching her without her realizing it.

Calming down, she said quietly, "I'm sorry. You lost someone close to you and I should be more respectful of your feelings."

Dex nodded decisively. She saw his lips were pressed tight together as if he was keeping himself from saying anything else.

Ramona could only imagine what he wasn't saying ran along the lines of:

Damn straight;

You should be, you killed her;

I had to face her parents, you didn't;

You broke up with me; I had every right to get with somebody else.

Ramona sighed. This was going to be harder than she thought.

After driving a while in silence, Ramona couldn't take it anymore. "Can I plug in my phone and listen to a playlist?"

Dex shrugged as he said, "Sure. Go ahead."

Listening to music helped relax the tension between them, but it didn't help her figure out what they could talk about now that catching up about the last year was a bad idea.

70

Suddenly, she caught sight of something that made her exclaim, "Hey! What's that?"

Dex slowed down and craned his head to look over through her side window.

"That is the Blayne estate," he told her.

The Blayne estate was located on a large tract of land, set well back from the road. For some reason, it stood out to her like it was much closer.

"Can we do a drive-by or something?"

Dex nodded. "Sure, but not too close. We don't want to intrude on the family while they are mourning."

He took a right and headed down the road for a mile or so before pulling over and shutting off the engine.

She rolled down her window and just stared. From where they were, she could see the house and the surrounding grounds. There were several smaller buildings scattered around the main house, primarily to the side and rear.

"What do you see?" Dex asked, curious.

"I don't know. It's a large house but so far back from the road, I shouldn't have really taken notice of it, but I did. Something about it caught my attention."

"Now, closer, it seems out of place; weird. I'm starting to feel weird. I feel like something is going to happen, but it's just a house. It isn't going to move or get up and walk away. It's fascinating for no reason." She glanced over at Dex.

He had a slight smile on his face. Embarrassed, she said, "Never mind. Let's go."

"Ramona, it's okay. I know what you mean, and I'm impressed. Usually, someone who isn't aware or 'in the know' can't see anything at all. They drive past the house like it isn't there. Or if they do see it, they have the opposite reaction; they want to stay away since they find it 'creepy'.

"You are feeling the power bound within. After generations of worship, there is a lot of power amassed in this area, in general, and in that estate, in particular."

"You are seeing the power of the worshipers living in the house. The house itself has absorbed the residual power of the many incantations and minor rituals performed there. The grounds are riddled with the various wards the family has placed over time."

"Uh, okay, but how can I or anyone else see power?"

Dex sighed. "You aren't seeing anything with your eyes in the visual spectrum. 'Sensing' would be a better word. It's nothing like you have ever experienced before and your mind is having a difficult time processing the sensory input; so, it looks off and you feel weird."

"Humans are relational beings, but where the mythos is involved, there isn't anything the brain can relate to. As such, most humans reject what they sense because they can't process the input."

"You are different. You don't understand, but you seem to be capable of accepting the input."

"As I said, I'm impressed," he finished, smiling again.

# Chapter Three

They got back on the road and about an hour later, Dex said, "We are almost there."

Ramona perked up, excited to see Dex's family house. She got her first look as they started down the long drive on the grounds of the estate.

It wasn't anything like she expected. It was a nice enough house; certainly larger than anything she had ever been in before. It seemed in fairly good repair, too, but it was somehow lacking.

Ramona was getting used to not understanding what she felt. Encouraged by what Dex had said earlier, she let her mind wander, to give it time to process. An image of a spent firecracker flashed in her mind briefly, and then she suddenly remembered a street from her old neighborhood. Ramona was confused at the conflicting images and also didn't get the connection between the house in front of her and a street from her past.

Before she could figure it out, Dex suddenly stopped the van and got out. Ramona did, too, even though they were still a good distance away from the house. He stared for a while without saying anything, then she heard him start to chant in a low, barely audible voice.

Nothing happened.

This seemed to upset him even more. With a sound of exasperation, he turned his back on the house, arms around his head in frustration.

*What in the world is with him?* she thought, as she watched him in silence.

She wondered if whatever he saw was related to the negative 'blowback' from the failed ritual.

When he turned back, his face was angry, eyes hard, and his teeth were clenched. Worried, she asked, "Dex, what's the matter? What's wrong?"

He took a breath as if he was going to answer, but only gestured angrily and glared at the house.

Taking charge, she said, "Okay. Calm down. I understand you are upset, and you can't explain it to me right now." She was using her nurse's voice and it seemed to help; he stopped glaring at the house. Nursing had been her other major.

"Do you want to go in?"

Dex shook his head.

"Okay. Let's go then."

Surprised, Dex found his voice, "Really? You are okay leaving after we drove all this way?"

"Yes. You are upset and if leaving will help, then we will go. I've got some money; we can find a hotel or something. I don't care, we'll find something."

Dex didn't answer, he just walked back to the van and got in. Ramona quickly did the same.

After leaving the grounds, Dex drove for a while before turning off the road to stop at a small grocery store.

"I've got somewhere in mind, but we should get some food and other stuff," Dex told her.

More curious than anything else, Ramona shopped with Dex. She insisted on paying for the groceries as he hadn't let her pay for gas earlier.

Back in the van, Ramona was getting tired. Dex was much calmer and she had had enough of being driven around. He took them off the main roads and down a gravel road for several miles; how far, she had no idea.

Finally, he pulled up to a small cabin. She got out and looked around. Born in the city, it felt strange to be out in the woods. Even more so now because the last time she had been in the woods like this, it was as Carlton's sacrifice.

Dex led the way up the stairs and opened the door. Going in, he turned on the light and then stood aside to let Ramona enter.

"Here we are. Will you be okay here for tonight?" he asked.

She walked into the main room and looking around said, "Yeah, sure. This is kind of nice actually. Much nicer than I thought a cabin in the woods would be."

"Good. I've had enough driving for one day."

"Me too. Let's get the stuff inside."

Together, they brought in the groceries and a couple of bags of clothes and other stuff from their dorm rooms.

While Dex put the groceries away, Ramona wandered around the cabin. It was more than nice; it was great. She had expected loose floorboards and a wet smell; that was her idea of a cabin in the woods.

It was one level, with a covered porch on two sides. The living/dining area had a fireplace in the corner. It opened into the kitchen. On the right of the main room, down a short hall, was a full bathroom and linen closet. The little hallway ended in a T-junction with another hallway. That hallway led to a master bedroom with its own bathroom and two smaller bedrooms.

Ramona went back into the main area and sat down on the couch. She was tired of sitting but was uncertain about what to do or say next. She eyed the fireplace, wishing it was cold enough to make a fire.

# Homecoming

Dex came over and sat down near her on the couch. He closed his eyes as he leaned back.

Ramona sat, staring at Dex. She was conflicted. He looked tired, so she wanted to give him some space but the list of things they were supposed to talk about was growing instead of getting shorter.

She decided she was compromising by asking him, "So, what is this place?"

Opening his eyes, he told her, "It's a prep place. There is a ritual site not too far from here. The Priests and more experienced practitioners use it as a base on the day before their ritual. The rest of us are supposed to use it as a place for study and practice. It gets used for the usual parties and stuff, too." Dex shrugged, as if it were no big deal, but she could see he was tense, and he wasn't looking at her.

"It's open to anyone?"

"No, not just any of us. Certain families have more rights or privileges than others, but the Phillips are on the shortlist, so it's okay for us to be here. Amongst us, if there isn't an upcoming ritual, it's on a first-come-first-serve basis."

"So, Dexter Phillips, you come from a family of privilege?" she asked, in a slightly amused tone.

He smiled at her and said, "Yeah." He was about to say more but his face suddenly got dark and he stopped talking.

Annoyed, she got up and walked across the room. Turning back to him, she asked, "What kind of privacy can we expect here? I mean, are we going to get kicked out? Is someone going to walk in whenever they feel like it?"

"Uh, well, normally, yes; it's a group house with lax rules. *But*, I did bring you up here to talk and that means we should have a certain amount of privacy." He got up from the couch and went over to one of his boxes on the floor. Rummaging around, he said, "I can ward others off."

"Do you really mean a ward or are you just going to put a tie on the doorknob?" she asked, slightly sarcastic.

Dex got up with a handful of things and a mischievous grin on his face and just said, "Yes."

Her curiosity of the mythos was stronger than her need to know what he had to tell her. Intrigued, she eagerly said, "Cool! Show me!"

# Chapter Four

They went outside where Dex showed her how to draw the warding symbols on the door and explained what to chant. Once she got the cadence right, they walked around the house chanting three times. When they got to the front door, Dex put his hand on top of hers and laid it flat over the symbol. Ramona felt a surge and then a kind of tingle.

Letting go of her hand, he said, "And that is how you do a basic warding. It's not very strong, so it won't keep much out, but it is enough to serve the purpose. Those in the know will go no further."

Pausing briefly, he continued, "So, how do you feel?"

Tired and energized at the same time, she said, "Hungry! Elated! Tired. Mostly hungry. We didn't really have lunch and it's late afternoon."

"Yeah, the lower and mid-range stuff is kind of fun. I can teach you more, if you want," he offered.

She glared at him, suddenly annoyed with him again. "Dexter. You are stalling and I've had enough."

She went inside and Dex followed meekly behind her.

Once inside, she turned towards him, frustrated and irritated, and said, "I know it's hard and I know you are tired, but there isn't going to be a good time, is there? I've tried to be patient, but you aren't even trying. Are you going to talk to me or not?"

Equally frustrated, Dex replied, "No. Yes! I mean, no, there is never going to be a 'good' time and, yes, I do want to tell you."

"It's just that I like that we are getting along; I like that you know as much as you do about me and it's great that you are kind of getting into practicing, too."

"I don't want it to end, which I'm worried it will when I tell you about my family."

Taking charge again, Ramona took him by the hand and led him over to the table. "Sit. I'll make something for us to eat while you talk. Just start talking. The sooner you start, the sooner it will be done."

Dex sat, slumped in the chair, eyes down, while she went to the fridge and got a couple of beers. She handed him one and then went back into the kitchen and started looking through the cabinets.

After a minute, he still hadn't said anything.

Ramona sighed. "Okay, I'll start with a brief recap about what I know about you, Dexter Phillips."

"You come from old money, you are an only child, you don't get along with your parents, you are a former drug user, you don't like your house, you are a skilled practitioner, and you worship Cthulhu."

She looked at Dex expecting a reaction when she pronounced the deity's name correctly but, nothing. His face was neutral, and his jaw was tight.

She continued making dinner as she went on in a more serious tone. "I know there are sacrifices. It's as normal to you like hunting is to others, or maybe more in the way farm kids are brought up on cattle farms. Rituals are just part of your life."

"I know you said you've participated in rituals and that you have done the…" She faltered, unsure how to say it.

"Killing," Dex filled in for her in a flat tone.

## Homecoming

*Friggin' hell.* And they were just getting started.

She put a lid on the pot and turned the burner down.

Coming over to the table, she sat down, beer in hand. "Have you ever been out of this area? I mean, do you know what it's like outside of your little bubble? I know this is your turf and all that, but have you ever been anywhere else?"

Dex sat up straight, reacting to her tone. It was nothing like he had ever heard her use before. It was strong and had a cold edge.

She went on, "I come from the city, the part people don't like to talk about. What you *think* you know about where I come from, is what you learned from watching TV shows."

"You know nothing. Out there, it's about dominance and pride, passion and blood. You live on the edge every day not because you are an adrenaline junkie, but because you know you aren't going anywhere. Tomorrow is going to be the same as today; nothing is ever going to change. You love without reservation or shame because when they leave, they might not come back."

"I've seen how cruel people can be to each other. I've known violence and I've known killers. Killing and death were a part of my life before I met you."

"I get it; you have killed people in sacrifice to your God. But from what I've seen, you are not like the brutal killers I have known."

"I get the 'why.' A hunger for power is nothing new to me. The lack of fear and brutality is different. The *civility* of it all is what is strange to me. I also see the order, the structure of your worship. From where I came from its just about mindlessly following 'the rules.' Rules that are basic, brutal, and ultimately so very pointless."

Dexter stunned, just sat and stared at her.

Ramona got up and went into the kitchen. When she came back, she had a pot of spaghetti and meatballs.

"Why don't you get us some plates and silverware?" she suggested.

Dex took a healthy swig of beer before getting up and going into the kitchen.

Sitting down again, he said, "I guess I never asked about you."

"Born in the city, never knew my father, mother died in a car wreck. I avoided foster care by crashing on whatever couch I could find until I turned 18. I sold anything we owned to get cash. I got a full scholarship to Derleth U and moved out here with practically nothing. The rest you know. Now quit stalling and talk."

Dex preferred her nurse voice to her current snide tone.

He inhaled through his nose and let it out again in a rush. He helped himself to a plateful of spaghetti and meatballs as he said, "Okay, yeah, about me. You didn't get as much right as you think you did."

"My family didn't come from money. My grandfather had nothing when he got to this county. He eventually made a fortune, but he *earned* it."

"He was a great man and a master practitioner. He trained my mother and eventually me. When it was time, he chose me to be the one to assist the High Priest. And what I mean is, he chose to be a sacrifice and he chose me to be the one who stood with the High Priest when she completed the ritual. I was fourteen."

"My parents had two children—me and my older sister, Anna. They sacrificed her when I was sixteen. You talk about loving like they may never come back, what is worse is loving like they will, and then they don't."

"I wasn't told anything about it. I was away, I can't even remember why now, and when I got back, she was gone. Just *gone*. No good-byes; nothing. Just lies. My father said she wanted it. He said it was her choice."

# Homecoming

"They even had cleaned out her room by the time I got back, but I knew where she hid her journal. Her last entry talked about how she would tell me she got to participate in a ritual and how jealous I would be."

"I was so angry with them. I turned my back on them and nearly everything I had been taught. My parents had to send me away again for the better part of two years. I came home for only several months before I left again for college."

Dex paused to finish chewing, then continued.

"After my first year at Derleth, I come home for the summer, and my father told me my mother was gone. No lies this time, but he didn't tell me anything either. He swore she wasn't sacrificed, and I believed him only because he refused to have a funeral."

"After that, I completely stopped worshipping; I quit practicing. I chose an additional major because it kept my mind on other things. Chemistry was too easy though. Once you've studied the esoteric, the world of science with its set laws and predicable outcomes is nothing. I got high because it felt good, but never as good as when I practiced."

"I met you and everything seemed right. I thought we were great together until you dumped me over some drugs that I never cared much about in the first place."

Dex finished his meal and pushed his plate back.

"I tore up my room and decided to get clean. After that, I got back into practicing, into worshipping."

"I pretty much picked up where I left off, as far as studying the mythos and worshipping Cthulhu, however, my father and I still don't get along."

"More recently, I knew that Carlton was going to perform his first ritual as High Priest. I knew Darla was his Chosen One, but I didn't know you were her roommate."

"When I found out, I tried to prevent you from being a sacrifice, but you ran away from me. Apparently, they caught you because the next time I saw you, Carlton was leading you both to the altar. And yes, I would have let you die. You know why? Because once a ritual starts, it *shouldn't* be stopped. You can't save lives once you've wakened the Dreamer."

He stopped speaking and gauged her reaction. The arrogant, 'I've seen it all' expression was gone from her face. She was shocked, but it wasn't as bad as he feared.

"More spaghetti?" he asked her.

# Chapter Five

"No, thank you, I've had enough," Ramona replied, automatically.

"You haven't eaten anything."

Surprised, she looked down at her plate. Seeing it was full, she picked up her fork and ate without speaking.

She was trying to take in everything Dex had just told her. It was difficult, not because of what he said, but also because of what he *didn't* say. He completely glossed over getting with that other girl. She was angry at herself for getting hung up on that when he had just bared his soul to her. *Dammit*, didn't she have any compassion?

When she was done eating, she got up abruptly and started clearing the table.

"Are you okay?" he asked her.

"I don't know. I'm upset and angry." Seeing the look on his face, she clarified quickly, "For you. I'm upset and angry for what they did to you. I'm not angry *at* you." She decided a little glossing might be a good thing after all.

"I'm not going to steal the keys and run off, if that is what you are worried about. Your family is or was a piece of work. What they did to you and your sister was horrible and cruel. I am *so* not looking forward to meeting your dad now."

"I should probably take some time to process, but right now I don't feel that differently about you." She turned her back and started to load the dishwasher.

Dex settled back against his chair, sipping at his beer. He knew this Ramona. Talking *was* her way of processing.

She went on. "I can see why you lost your faith, so to speak. Well maybe. Sacrificing a family member is normal, isn't it?"

Shaking his head, he replied, "No, not so much in a family of prestige. It happens more in families who have to earn their stripes. And if the family does take an unwilling sacrifice, it's usually the spouse, not one of the children."

"You are making a distinction between willing and unwilling," she interjected.

"I am. It made a difference that my grandfather was willing; that he chose to give himself to Cthulhu."

"How so?"

"Several ways. It was a rite of passage for me. It was also a passing of the torch, so to speak, from him to my mother, who was the High Priest in the ritual. We gave him to Cthulhu, yes, but in doing so, his power moved through us first."

"In this case, the ritual made us stronger and united us as a family."

Ramona left the kitchen but didn't join him at the table. Instead, she flopped down on the couch. Dex got up and sat down at the end, facing her.

"So, that couldn't be what your parents were doing, when they took your sister? I mean, that made your family less, not more, right?" she asked.

"Right. I don't know what they were doing. I do think something went wrong; that it backfired somehow."

"I saw it for the first time just this afternoon. Something isn't right about my family, my house. I don't think it's been right since they killed Anna. I don't know; maybe I was too angry or inexperienced to see it before now, or maybe it has just got worse over time."

"How weak my family is really hit me after seeing my house right after we left the Blayne estate. Even after losing Carlton, they are every bit as strong as they were before."

Ramona was dubious. "How does seeing houses tell you all that?"

Dex smiled faintly. "Sorry; don't take me literally. 'House' has a different meaning in my crowd. Are you familiar with personal auras and how mediums claim to be able to see a person's aura and be able to predict their future?"

Ramona nodded, saying, "Yes, sure."

"One's house is like a family's aura, especially in families who have worshipped for generations. Normally, the family estate, their physical house, is the locus, the seat of their power."

"Okay, I get that, but what were you doing by chanting?"

Dex thought for a moment. "It was a summoning incantation of a lesser creature and it didn't work. I was using the incantation as a test. I don't know how to explain it but it's like the house is drained or used up."

Ramona thought of the image that came to her when she looked at the house. Thinking about the used firecracker, she asked, "It's dead, then?"

"No, death is a release and it has an energy of a sorts. What I saw is not dead, but it's not alive either."

Ramona shuddered, "I can see why you had to get out of there. I wouldn't like to see my aura that messed up either."

She thought of the other image, the street near where her mother and she had lived. What was her brain trying to tell her? It was just a street.

*Oh hell.* Ramona suddenly got the reference. That street was the one both rival gangs claimed was in their territory. They fought over it every once in a while.

Dex was watching her, looking puzzled, but waited for her to speak.

"Dex, could it be that your parents are fighting something? That would explain why your summoning failed. I mean, maybe it *did* work, but the creature wouldn't come anywhere near the house. Kind of like a guy without colors isn't going to get in between two gangs going at it."

Dex didn't say anything, so she went on. "You must have summoned something small, something that might have been afraid of something bigger than it? Is that possible? If they were fighting something, could that have something to do with what happened to your mother? And why your 'house' is so spent?"

Dex had gone pale as he considered what she was saying.

"I..I don't know. If they were, if there is, they would have told me," he stammered. He didn't sound confident.

She reached over to take his hand tightly in hers, saying, "I'm sorry; I don't mean to upset you. I'm sure I have no idea what I'm talking about."

Dex, his eyes on hers, only nodded. He took a deep breath and swallowed, trying to loosen his throat.

Grimacing slightly, she said, "Thank you for finally telling me."

Dex, sensing a moment, leaned over and kissed her.

Ramona kissed him back. She had missed him, and he had just shared so much with her.

Pulling back suddenly, she said, "No. I can't. Not like this. It's too soon." She got abruptly to her feet, saying "I'll take the middle room. Good night."

Dex was thinking, why not now, but only muttered a faint g'night, as he watched her leave the room.

# Homecoming

## Chapter Six

Ramona woke early the next morning. She shuffled out of her room and into the kitchen. After getting the coffee maker going, she headed into the bathroom for a shower.

By the time she got out, Dex was in the kitchen making breakfast. They exchanged 'good mornings' and she got herself a cup of coffee. Sitting down at the table, she watched him as she tried to figure out her feelings for him now that she knew all his secrets.

The first thing she realized was that she was still attracted to him and last night hadn't been just a heat of the moment thing. She still felt the same way she had when they were dating.

In fact, thoughts about making use of any of the three empty bedrooms were distracting her from fully processing what he had told her. She was annoyed with herself; they should be working out if there is something going on at his family's house, and not wasting time doing other things.

Dex finished what he was doing and came over to the table with two plates of eggs, bacon, and toast.

He took it as a good sign that she immediately started eating. "How did you sleep?"

"Good actually," she answered. "Better than I had been."

"The human mind can be very resilient if the person doesn't let themselves get hung up on what they assume can't be real or what doesn't make sense with their laws of nature or physics," Dex replied, ever the academic.

"Or if they don't let the morality of what they did bother them," she said, more to her plate, than to him.

Dex stopped eating and looked at her. He wasn't certain if she meant his actions and the taking of sacrifices, or her actions, that led to the death of many of his friends and colleagues.

"I mean, I want to let it go; I really do, but I feel like I should apologize or do something to atone. You know what I mean?" she asked.

Dex relaxed slightly; she was talking about her actions. This wasn't the first time Ramona had simply taken for granted what he would have considered to be the bigger issue. She seemed to be okay with the practice of ritual killing. If she was accepting of their, of his, practices, he was not going to argue.

He wondered if that was what was bothering her. Was what happened at the ritual upsetting her so much that it was keeping her from being with him?

"I think so," he answered slowly, "but do you mean make it up to me or make things right in terms of the negative blowback from your part in the failed ritual?"

She simply said, "Yes," with a slight smile that was meant to remind him of his habit of responding to two questions with a single word.

He didn't smile back. "How serious are you? I mean, really? And how serious are you about learning the ways of our worship?"

"I am serious about making it up to you. That I'm sure of. But, how serious do I have to be about learning more?" she asked.

"There is a ritual I can show you how to perform, if you want. *If* done correctly, you will appease Cthulhu. However, in doing so, you will bring yourself to his attention again and he will not forget you. Think of it as an initiation that you cannot go back from; only forward."

"And you? Will you and I be okay if I do this?" she pressed.

Dex paused to give himself time to really consider his feelings. Deep down, he was angry at her for her part in the failed ritual. Even as much as he wanted to be with her, he did need something more than just apologies.

"Yes. But don't think you have to do this because of me. I would not make you do this as any sort of condition to be together or anything like that."

Looking at him steadily she replied, "I understand; *I* want to do it."

# Chapter Seven

Dex trained Ramona over the next two days. He explained the ritual and was very clear that it would require her blood to complete.

Once she agreed, he gave her the chants to study and made her write them down in a journal he gave her. Dex told her all the practitioners keep a journal.

On the morning of the third day, Dex led her through the woods to the ritual site. He was dressed in robes, but she was not. He assured her that what she was wearing was fine. In fact, she first had to earn the right to wear a robe.

Once there, Dex began chanting in a low drone. Ramona felt the power gathering. Focusing, she began the first of her chants while drawing the symbols and then laying out the items on the altar stone. Now that she was chanting, the power surged through her. It was invigorating and a little distracting.

Like before, the world around her suddenly changed. It was no longer cool and damp. She could still hear and see Dex behind her, but outside of the altar, it was dark. The air was hot and thick. She could see, but it wasn't the light of the rising sun. Mercifully, she didn't feel the ground breathing this time. Maybe it was because she was in charge of this ritual, or maybe Dex was anchoring them.

She had to fight to maintain her focus. Dex increased the intensity of his chant; it helped steady her.

Ramona began the second chant as she took the knife from the altar. An eye opened in the sky; *his* eye. Terror filled her as memories from the first ritual flooded her mind.

Reaching deep down within herself to find the will, she managed to keep chanting. Then with a clean, quick motion, she sliced her wrist and palm open. The blood flowed out of her and down onto the altar.

She looked up at the eye. It was watching her, but it was not angry like she remembered from before.

She let the blood continue to flow until the eye closed.

Looking down at the altar, she was surprised that the blood was neither pooling nor spilling over the edge.

A form began to emerge nearby. As it became more evident, Ramona could see the creature had some sort of weird wings and a long tongue or nose. The tongue was sucking her blood from the stone. *Ewwwwww.*

Dex kicked the back of her leg with his foot. Getting a hold of herself, Ramona began the third and final chant. She laid the knife down and took the cloth from the altar, covering the gash she had made. Automatically, she raised her arm and applied pressure to stop the bleeding.

Just as suddenly as they left, they were back in the woods. The air was again thin and cool. Gratefully, she sucked it in, breathing hard. She was light-headed and tired but elated at the same time.

Still applying pressure, she turned around to face Dex.

"How did I do?" she asked him, a little woozy from turning too quickly.

He pulled the cowl back from his face and said, "You did great. How do you feel?"

"Good. Tired. Better, I think. Maybe it's the adrenaline, but I don't have that sick feeling that something bad is going to happen anymore," she answered, still panting a little.

Dex smiled briefly, and said, "C'mon. Let's get back to the cabin and dress your hand."

Once there, Dex cleaned and dressed her wound with an expertise that initially surprised her. Then she shrugged it off, assuming learning how to handle minor wounds was part of their basic training.

After her hand was wrapped, Ramona sat at the table, intently watching Dex as he packed up the first aid kit. "Now what?" she asked him.

"Do you want to lie down? You're probably tired. I can make you something to eat if you are hungry."

The thought of lying down with Dex appealed to her. "I'm not hungry for food." She leaned over and kissed him.

He kissed her back before pulling away.

"No, we probably shouldn't. I know what you are feeling, and I don't want to take advantage of you. We should wait."

Ramona sat back against her chair; lips tight.

"I appreciate your thoughtfulness."

She stood up and walked out of the main room, toward the bedroom. A moment later he saw her shirt come from around the corner and land on the floor.

Dex was not unaffected by the ritual they had just performed nor from the events from the past several weeks that had been very difficult for him, as well. He got up and joined her in the bedroom.

# Chapter Eight

Later in the afternoon, Ramona and Dex lay together on the couch. Their dinner of hamburgers was grilling on the rack in the fireplace. They each had a beer. Dex was reading one of his books and Ramona was doing something with her phone.

Tired, Dex closed his book and looked down at Ramona, who was curled up against him. It was like before they broke up, but even better. She knew all about him now.

As he stretched, she leaned forward to take her weight off him and settled back down against him when he finished.

"Hey," she said looking up at him with a smile.

"Hey," he returned, also smiling. "What are you looking at? I didn't think we have a good cell signal in the cabin."

"I'm not online. I'm looking at Curwen's journal."

Dex jumped so suddenly he spilled his beer. "What!? Are you serious? How did you get that?" he exclaimed.

Ramona knew Curwen had been Carlton's ritual advisor. He had also survived Cthulhu's wrath and was the one Dex had to make a deal with to keep him quiet about her being at the failed ritual.

Ramona sat up to face him, saying, "It was the night of the ritual. After I ran away from you, I went to Carlton's dorm room by way of the fire escape. If you remember, he had

Darla and I didn't know where he was going to take her. I went to his room to see what I could find out."

"With you so far. Go on."

"Curwen's suitcase and satchel were there in his room. I searched them and found the journal. It was really interesting. It was old and written in different languages. It was hand-bound with old and new paper."

As she paused, Dex nodded for her to go on.

"Well, I knew I couldn't take it, but I wanted to study it more, so I took pictures of the pages with my phone."

"I'm looking to see how they came out. I had forgotten I had them until you gave me my own journal to write in."

"Damn! You have no idea what someone would pay to get hold of something as valuable as Joseph Curwen's journal."

Ramona was dubious. "Really? Why? It doesn't say much. And who is Joseph Curwen anyway? He seemed really creepy to me."

Dex made a face at her use of the word 'creepy'.

Remembering creepy could be synonymous with power, she made a face back, and asked, "So who is he besides being a practitioner, like you?"

Dex shook his head. "No, not like me. He is way above my level. He is also an amoral, sadistic total bastard."

"May I see?" Dex asked, suddenly polite.

Surprised at his vehemence, as well as his incongruent request, Ramona handed him her phone. Dex swiped through the images until he came to pages that were not written in the free form style of a diary entry. She couldn't read the text very well, but the style was almost that of a recipe.

"These are his notes and incantations. Even though every practitioner has to formulate his own, we copy bits and pieces from others where we can," Dex told her.

"So, what makes it valuable then?"

"It helps to know where others have gone before, and the more skilled the practitioner, the higher the quality of the bits and pieces that can be gleaned."

"What is strange is it doesn't seem to be written in code or in any archaic language," he mused, almost to himself.

Curious, she asked, "Why would it be?"

"Eh. Most of us aren't really good at sharing our knowledge outside our family, and sometimes not even with our family."

"The pages are not in order. When it was rebound, some pages were mixed up. Would that be on purpose?" she asked.

"Canny, diabolical old man!"

Not following, Ramona asked, "Why is that so clever? And he didn't look old to me."

"Think of the incantations like a set of instructions. If the instructions for how to program a DVR are mixed with the ones to program a nuclear warhead, you will figure it out. It's too big a leap not to notice."

"But what if you are dealing with an area of knowledge that is much less known or understood? Then, the two sets of instructions might seem to fit."

"If you were to try and follow the instructions, who knows what would happen. You might not get anything. Or you might have thought you were summoning a lesser creature and end up bringing forth a stronger creature, one that you were unprepared to deal with. A whole host of things could happen; very bad, awful things."

"Wow. That is diabolical!" she exclaimed. "But why did you call him old," she asked again.

"Curwen was born sometime in the 1600s. He isn't in his original body," Dex answered. He tried not to hold his breath, but he hoped she wouldn't realize that he had helped Curwen with his last body transfer ritual.

Partly because he wanted to distract her and partly because he wanted to know, he asked, "If you know the pages are out of order, does that mean you know which pages belong together?"

"I think so, some of them anyway."

"Will you be willing to show me?" he asked excitedly.

"Sure," Ramona agreed as if it was no big deal.

The two worked through dinner and into the night. They had always enjoyed studying together and this subject was particularly interesting to them both.

--------------------

Waking up on the couch the next day, Ramona groaned as she felt the knot in her neck.

Dex wasn't with her on the couch and she didn't see him anywhere in the room or in the kitchen. She got up and went to the bathroom, trying to stretch her neck out as she walked.

When she got out, she looked in the bedrooms. No Dex.

Peering out the windows, she saw him standing outside on the porch. As she went outside, she shivered in the chill of the early morning. The porch was cold on her bare feet.

Walking softly, she went over and put her arms around him from behind and just hugged him without saying anything. He seemed sad and lost in thought.

"I have to go," Dex said. His voice was husky with emotion.

Ramona knew, but asked anyway, "Where? Go where?"

"Home. Back home. It's time I faced it; them. Everything I've been running away from for so long." Dex grasped her hands tightly.

"We'll go together."

"No." His flat, determined tone surprised her.

Turning to face her, he said, "Ramona, I don't know what I'll find. You may be right; there may be something in the house. If there is, it's in deep trouble. I can't promise I will be able to protect you."

"You need my help," she insisted.

"I need you, yes. I need you safe," he whispered, eyes dark with emotion.

"I need you, too,' she whispered back gently.

Suddenly changing her tone, "I'm coming. You need someone to have your back."

"Ramona, please. I didn't want to have to say this, but you are only a neophyte. You are more vulnerable than you realize."

"Hey, I've *already* graduated to a neophyte. I'm making progress. Does that mean I get to wear a robe now?"

"And, doesn't every Priest need a cantor, I mean, chanter? I'm a back-up power source for you. You might need that," she argued.

She could see him wavering. "I understand the risks. You don't know what you are facing but I could help tip the odds in your favor."

He sighed in resignation. "I should have sacrificed you when I had the chance."

# Chapter Nine

It took the rest of the morning to pack and clean up the cabin. Dex did most of it because he wanted her to read the sections of his journal dealing with wards and protection incantations. While she practiced writing symbols, he went through the boxes of his stuff for things to put in his backpack. He gave her several items to put in her backpack, as well. She, ever practical, also packed sandwiches and bottles of water.

When it was time to go, Dex looked sad at leaving the cabin. Ramona, however, was not. While she had enjoyed their time together, she felt they were moving forward towards something, rather than hiding away. She didn't like hiding. She preferred a confrontation every time.

It did worry her, a little, that Dex was not more confident about going home; as if he didn't like their chances. She decided it was only more reason for her to be there for him.

Back in the van, en route to the Phillips estate, Ramona was excited and ready for anything.

"Hey, shouldn't we rehearse my back story? How we met and all that, in case your father asks? I was Darla's roommate; will he wonder about that, too?"

Dex was hesitant, but finally said, "No, it's okay. I don't think it will come up. He will be very happy to see you; he won't have many questions."

Ramona was silent as she tried to work out what Dex wasn't telling her.

"Oh! He'll just think I'm your Chosen. He won't care about any of my details, will he?" she asked, suddenly getting it.

"Right."

"But, I'm not. Don't you plan on telling him that?" Her tone was more accusing than she meant it to be. She wasn't nervous about being sacrificed; she was more concerned about why he wouldn't tell his father they were a serious couple.

"Ramona, please. First things first, He and I have barely spoken in years. We're hardly going to have a father and son moment over you."

"Oh, yeah. Right. Sorry."

"Stay focused, please," he chided her.

Dex took the time during the rest of the trip to review the layout of the house and grounds. As they pulled up, he reminded her to stay alert and to trust her instincts.

This time, he drove directly up to the front of the house and parked. As he got out, he slung his backpack over his shoulder and slammed the van door defiantly.

Ramona took her time. Standing at the base of the steps, she looked curiously up at the house. As she did, she felt a tingle along the back of her neck. She gave her brain time to process, to see if it would tell her anything.

She didn't get any images, but she did hear the whistling sound from the old westerns when two gunfighters squared off.

*Oh great.*

She hurried to catch up to Dex, up the porch stairs and into the house, then through an entrance hallway, and finally into a very grand foyer. She stopped dead and looked around. Maybe it was a rotunda, but whatever it was called, it had a spiral staircase that led up towards an ornate domed ceiling.

## Homecoming

She sternly told herself to quit gawking and focus. Dex was standing in the center of the foyer/rotunda, eyes shut, concentrating.

Ramona scanned the area, alert, in case something rushed at them. She had no idea why she was suddenly so hyped up, but her heart was racing.

Taking a deep breath, she closed her eyes and focused like Dex was doing. Once she did, she immediately felt a presence.

Something that couldn't be seen by her eyes, something that counted on using that limitation to trick her into thinking nothing was there. A chill went through her. She was scared but knew better than to run.

Dex began chanting; she didn't recognize what. Remembering her position as a neophyte to the Priest, she began to chant, too. Dex had some fancy name for the chant, but she just called it the All-Purpose Grounding Chant. Whatever the name, it should help Dex with whatever he was doing.

She felt an eerie tingle up her spine. Another presence? Before she could figure out for sure, she felt a jolt, like something near her had been hit, hard. Both presences were suddenly gone.

Ramona stopped chanting when she heard Dex stop. Cautiously opening her eyes, she looked around. Dex had his eyes open and was looking at her. He seemed drained, but he nodded at her.

"Thank you, that was very helpful," he told her, his voice tired.

"What was that?" she asked, trying to sound matter of fact.

Dex shook his head, a grave expression on his face. "No idea."

"Dexter! How good it is to see you!" a large voice boomed from above.

Looking up, she saw a man peering over the railing on the second floor.

"Father. How good it is for you to welcome me home," Dex called back.

The man, presumable Charles Phillips, grimaced. After an awkward pause he said, "And you have brought a friend; how nice. Welcome, my dear. Welcome to *my* house."

Ramona wondered at his phrasing. Why did he feel it necessary to say stress that?

"I'll see you in the library presently," Mr. Phillips called down curtly before disappearing from sight.

Ramona looked at Dex, "What was *that* all about?"

He shrugged. "I'm not sure. He's been like that for a while; I try and not let it get me, but sometimes he just gets under my skin. C'mon. I'll show you around."

He was making signs like he wanted to show her around, but she saw he was tense, and his eyes were wary.

She followed him. Getting in close, she whispered, "Dex, I think it's important. Why is he insecure about the house? Or as you say, the family power bank?"

Dex stopped walking. "Go on."

"You told me that your grandfather built this house, right? Your maternal grandfather?"

She went on as Dex nodded. "And he made it a point to give it to your mother and *you*. Was your father part of the ritual?"

Dex shook his ahead. From his expression, he was starting to get where she was going.

"So, if she is no longer here, the house is more yours than his? Unless there a will?"

"Not necessarily. He has a claim to it. He was my mother's husband and he is my father, my elder. I don't know about a will. It has never been discussed, but he's never admitted she is dead."

"I get what you are saying, and if you are right, in my mother's absence, he and I share a dual claim on the house and everything in it."

"Is this important? I mean, does it matter?"

Dex was silent for a time as he thought about it. Finally, he said, "It wouldn't matter if he and I were on the same side. It would be important if we were on a different or opposing side."

Ramona inhaled deeply and held it for a moment as she considered the implications. She let it out in exasperation and asked, "So why hasn't he challenged you or otherwise had it out with you?"

Dex shrugged saying, "I have no idea." Seeing her bite her lip, he asked, "Do you?"

"Well, I don't know, but from what you told me, he probably wouldn't win. If he killed his daughter and lost his wife that would be detriments to his power, wouldn't it? You, on the other hand, are rising, gaining knowledge and power. Well, now that you are 'back,' I mean have started practicing again."

"Actually...", she started saying then stopped herself.

"Actually?" Dex pressed.

"Did he try and stop you from leaving the family or encourage you to keep practicing after you 'lost' your mother?"

Dex sucked in his breath, and answered, "No. You're suggesting he wants me gone."

"I don't know! It could mean anything. If your parents were fighting something, maybe they just wanted you out of the house and safe. *But*, I do think we need to figure out what is going on before either of us is the next sacrifice."

# Chapter Ten

Dex grabbed her hand, saying, "C'mon. The first place to start would be my mother's study." He led her up the stairs while she tried not to gawk at the domed ceiling.

Opening the door, he led her inside the room and switched on the light. It was huge. It looked like a professor's study with books lining the shelves and even a large blackboard with writing and symbols. There was a fireplace on the right wall.

Wandering around Ramona asked Dex, "What does this mean?", gesturing to the blackboard.

He looked at it a moment and said, "I don't know. I would need time to study it. Right now, I want to get her journal."

As he sat down at his mother's desk, Ramona took a picture of the blackboard with her phone.

"What are you doing in here? Get out immediately!" demanded Mr. Phillips.

Ramona jumped and quickly turned around. Mr. Phillips was standing in the doorway, looking very angry.

"I am giving Ramona a tour of the house," Dex replied, calmly. "Why don't you show her the dome? At this hour, the light should be shining through the stained glass."

Mr. Phillips glared at Dex. "No one should be in here. She wouldn't like it."

"I would like a minute, please. Won't you show Ramona the stained glass for me?" Dex was oddly calm.

## Homecoming

Ramona wondered if he always spoke to his father so formally.

Mr. Phillips's expression changed from angry to entreating, like he suddenly thought of something. His eyes now had a strangely vacant look. He turned to Ramona and said, "Yes, certainly. You are in for such a treat."

Ramona turned to glare at Dex. She was not happy at having to be the distraction or at having to be alone with Mr. Phillips.

Dex gave her a brief pleading look before shrugging as if to say, 'go on.'

Mr. Phillips walked her back out to the balcony as he started to tell her about the history of the stained glass. He sounded like one of her more boring professors; not at all the engaging academic like his son.

He walked around the circular perimeter of the balcony, talking all the while; talking on and on about the stained glass.

He was droning; she couldn't even understand him anymore. She suddenly felt groggy and didn't want to walk anymore. Stopping, she clutched at the railing with both hands, taking deep breaths to try and clear her head.

What was he saying? Look up? Look where?

Without warning, Mr. Phillips grabbed her and tried to push her over the railing. Misjudging her strength, he didn't break her hold on the railing. As they struggled, she head-butted him.

Was he still chanting? Without thinking, she drove her fist up hard into his gut with a vicious uppercut. Sucking wind, he doubled over.

She ran partway back to the study before stopping. She could still feel him in her head. Whatever he did to her was still there; she felt him in her mind. She hadn't really broken free from him.

Dex had told her that some creatures and particularly nasty practitioners can maintain a hold on their subject for years. Mr. Phillips hadn't gotten full control of her, but she wouldn't let him retain *any* hold over her.

Now more angry than scared, she steeled herself and walked back. He had straightened up but was still breathing heavily with a hand over his ribs.

"You little..", he began to say, but she didn't give him a chance to finish. She made a wide slashing motion, slicing his hand with a knife she pulled from her pocket.

"Release me!" she ordered.

"I can't; she wants you," he said in a pitiful tone. His voice was strained; almost like he was choking.

Without thinking, she sliced him again. He screamed and shouted, "I can't; she wants you."

"Ramona, stop!," Dex sternly ordered from behind her.

Breathing heavily, Ramona backed away and tried to get a hold of herself. It was all she could do to put down the knife.

"Father, release her and we can talk about Mother. Please." Dex's voice was gentle, but still commanding.

The two men stared at each other. It was evident that Mr. Phillips was struggling, but with what, wasn't evident.

Holding up a journal, Dex continued, "I know what happened to Mother and I know you need me now. Release Ramona and I can help."

Mr. Phillips's face contorted into a mixed expression of sadness and pride. He only said, "Dexter" before dropping what looked like a crystal pendant on the floor. Ramona felt the release as he crushed the pendant under his foot.

"Father, go dress your hand and lie down," Dex told his father, in a more compassionate tone, but still commanding.

"You know what happened. Help us end this!" Mr. Phillips said intensely, pleadingly.

Dex nodded solemnly. His father nodded back before walking away, clutching his cut hand to his chest.

Ramona waited until after he was gone before asking, "You do? From what, five minutes with her journal?" Ramona, still angry, was incredulous.

Dex glared at her. "No, of course not. I had to say something to stop you both from killing each other."

Still glaring, he added, "You know he's my father, right?"

She opened her mouth to argue, but she couldn't say anything as she took in what almost happened. She dropped her eyes briefly. Looking up at him she only nodded.

Dex didn't say anything as he watched her wipe the knife clean on her pant leg before closing the blade and slipping it back into her pocket.

As they walked back to the study, Ramona muttered, "He said she wants me."

Dex, uncertain, asked, "Why would she want you? For what?"

She didn't answer and Dex didn't say anything either. Once they were both in the study, he locked the door and sat down at his mother's desk and began to read her journal.

Ramona, still upset, felt like she was left hanging. Not that she wanted to argue with him, but, what the hell had just happened?

Realizing Ramona was watching him, Dex looked up and asked, "What?"

Gaping at him, she asked, "What?! What just happened?"

"I don't know; I'm trying to figure it out."

Ramona bit back a snarky reply. Seeing his hands were trembling, she realized he was just as upset as she was.

"How come you can read her journal? Shouldn't it be in code or something?" she asked instead.

"It is. She taught me the cipher. It is the same one her father taught her."

"And why are you just reading it now? You said she died years ago." Ramona still argumentative, tried to get a hold of herself.

"He told me she wasn't dead, and I wanted to believe him. If she was alive, she would never forgive me for reading her journal without her permission," Dex explained.

"So, you have been in some sort of limbo-like holding pattern for all this time? Not knowing what happened?"

When he nodded, she shuddered. "I know why you didn't come home much, especially with that thing in the hall."

"Stop. Say no more about 'that' unless you want to draw it you," he commanded sharply.

Her jaw dropped briefly before mouthing, "Really?"

Dex nodded. "Can I get on with trying to find out what happened now, please?"

She left him to it. She roamed around the study and browsed through his mother's eclectic collection of books and relics. She was puzzled about Dex. If it had been her mother, she would have fought like hell to find out what had happened. It was clear to her now that his father wouldn't have been of any help over the last couple of years. Why not tell Dex, his son, about 'that' thing? Why wait until he figured it out for himself? Worried, she got out several items from her backpack to draw and empower several warding signs around the room.

If Dex noticed, he didn't say anything. He just continued to read his mother's journal. Sometimes he would stop and puzzle over the incantation on the blackboard before returning to the journal.

Ramona distracted herself by looking at the books again.

Sometime later, she felt her stomach rumble in hunger. Checking the time, she saw that it was well after lunchtime.

## Homecoming

Before she could ask about dinner, Dex abruptly slammed his hands on the desk and leaned forward, holding his head in his hands.

Head still down, she heard him say in a muffled voice, "Well, at least I know what happened."

His shoulders began to shake as he cried softly. Ramona quickly went over and put her arms around him, holding him tightly against her.

When he finally looked up, he said, "We're in deep trouble."

# Chapter Eleven

Ramona struggled to control conflicting emotions. Something in his mother's journal had really upset him though, at the same time, she wanted to say, 'You think? It's not like your father didn't just try to kill me or anything'. Strangely, her instincts told her to be calm. Usually, instincts tell you to fight or flee. Hers was telling her to stay right where they were.

"Why do I feel safe here?"

Dex's eyebrows shot up at the unexpected question. "I don't know. This was my mother's study; it was my grandfather's before her."

"So, you are the third generation to sit here? In the center of your 'house'?"

"Yeah. Yes, I guess you could say so. I am here behind wards, with reinforcements, so you could say we are in a fairly well-protected bunker." He was a bit taken aback but appreciated the need for strategic thinking. He was almost glad she was here, if it wasn't for the situation they were in now.

"Can you tell me what happened?" she asked in her clinical, nurse's voice.

"You deserve to know, but I can only give you the short version." Dex sombered; he cleared his throat before he went on and tried to sound like an academic.

# Homecoming

"From what my mother wrote, they never intended for Anna to die. She wasn't meant to be a sacrifice. They were doing a ritual together, the three of them, but it went wrong. Horribly wrong."

Dex stopped to take a deep breath.

"They released a foul hideousness; an unseeable horror. They tried to fight it but it was too strong. It took Anna and wounded my mother when she tried to save her."

"My mother's wound did not heal. Whatever that foul thing was, it still had a hold on her. It stayed in the house and fed on her."

"That is why they didn't want you home!" Ramona exclaimed, interrupting him. "Your mother, your dad, they *were* protecting you!"

"Yes, but I was no neophyte then and am certainly not now! I should have been told! I should have been allowed to fight and avenge Anna!"

Ramona had never seen Dex so white-hot angry. Trying to calm things down, she switched back to using her clinical tone, and asked, "Did it come back for your mother? What happened next?"

"As I said, it was feeding on her; draining her. My father and she wanted to do an incantation to pray for power from beyond, so she could break its hold and rejuvenate herself."

"You mean a youth spell?" she asked.

"No, not a youth spell. Sometimes what is drained can't be fixed by a hot meal and good night's sleep. And, I think they wanted to make her stronger, so she could fight it."

"What went wrong?"

"*That* part isn't in the journal. What Mother did write was how 'it' was also trying to take over Philip, my father. When it got even partial control, it made him say and do things. He was getting weak; she was afraid he would lose control of himself or be driven insane by the creature. She, they, were desperate."

"Her last incantation is there on the blackboard. From what I can tell, it's right. It should have done what it was supposed to." Dex's voice was tired even though he still looked angry and frustrated.

Ramona took his hand. "We should take a break and eat. I have the food and water I put in my backpack. It isn't much, but it will help."

As they ate, Ramona stared at the blackboard and said, "Can you walk me through it? I've never seen spells before."

"It's not magic," he scolded her, "but I'll try."

Gesturing to the blackboard, he said, "This part opens the way to the void and this part invokes Cthulhu. Assuming he accepts, this third part draws the power into the Priest's body."

"How exactly was this incantation supposed to break 'its' hold?" she asked.

"With enough power, she would have been strong enough to possibly kill or at least drive it back to where it had been released from," Dex replied.

"Wouldn't she have to break its hold first, and then try and kill it?"

"Yeah, maybe. So?"

"Well, how do you break an incorporeal being's hold on a corporeal body? For that matter, how do you kill an incorporeal horror? Wouldn't they have to be on the same playing field? I mean, would it have to become corporeal or the Priest have to become incorporeal?"

The color drained from Dex's face as he stared, gaping at her before turning to look at the incantation. Finally, he said, "My mother didn't die. She *is* here; fighting that thing."

# Chapter Twelve

"What?! That's awful. How can we help her?" Ramona asked, always ready for a fight.

"Hold on. I have to think; there was a lot my mother said in her journal. I mean, we have to figure this out," Dex clarified. Ramona looked questionably at Dex; wondering why clarify such a point?

He mouthed, 'she said a LOT.'

Dex continued out loud, "I don't think we know everything we need to. We are only going to get one chance when we do make our move, so it better be the right one."

"We don't know where it can go or what it can 'hear'," he cautioned her, looking at her meaningfully.

*Oh*..."Great. That is going to make planning tough. Anyway, so if she wants me, that means it's your mother who wants me. Is that why your father tried to kill me?"

"Maybe. Maybe if he was being controlled at the time. But if he knows Mother is here, why isn't he helping her? And if he doesn't want me around, why did he agree with me that he needs my help?"

Ramona moaned in irritation and frustration. "How can we possibly find out? Your dad must know something is up by now, and we can't be sure if he is for or against us. Something is after us that two experienced practitioners couldn't defeat.

*And*, the one person who might be able to help, has no way of talking to us!"

Dex jumped slightly, "Wait! That isn't necessarily true. 'She wants you'. That is what he said!"

"Yeah, so? Wants me for what?" Ramona's body tensed even as her jaw dropped as she suddenly got it. "No, you can't mean she wants my body? Are you are going to give her my body?"

"What?! No! I couldn't do an interbody transfer even if I wanted to. For one thing, we're missing one of the bodies. *But*, if you are willing, you could be her temporary host," Dex finished in imploringly.

"How temporary?" Ramona was skeptical. She didn't want any arguments over ownership.

'Possession is nine-tenths of the law.'

*Friggin' hell!* Where did that thought come from? Was her brain trying to make a joke? That was assuming it was even her brain, her own thought. She couldn't be sure with two incorporeal entities running around.

"Just the length of the incantation," Dex was saying at the same time.

"Why didn't she just inhabit you sometime between her 'transformation' and now?"

"She's not a ghost. She can't just waft into somebody, like in the movies. It's a complicated process. And it would make things a lot easier for her if you invited her in, so to speak," he said, even now the academic.

She tried not to shudder at his phrasing. "*Promise* me I will get full and sole ownership back?"

"I *promise*," he assured her.

"Okay. But this is going to be really weird; me and your mother in the same body, sharing thoughts," she grumbled, making a face.

"You think I like it? You think I really want my *mom* to know me the way you do? I wouldn't ask if it wasn't absolutely necessary!" Dex growled, scowling at her.

"Okay, okay. What do we need to do?" she asked.

"Try and focus. I'll strengthen your wards and then, between some of my grandfather's books and Curwen's notes, I will come up with the incantation."

"What do I do?"

"Rest; it's going to take a lot out of you. Meditate, if you can, to clear your mind and to get yourself used to the idea of allowing her in."

After strengthening the wards, Dex got to work. Ramona laid down on the floor and tried to clear her mind. Suddenly, she sat up, asking, "Do you have any pictures of your mother? It might help if I had an idea of who she was."

Dex didn't answer, but he pulled out his phone and tapped for a moment before throwing it to her.

Ramona swiped through the pictures. At first, she thought it was nice and a little bit fun to see Dex with his family. They looked happy in a lot of the pictures. Julia, his mother, had been really pretty—when she had a body.

Juxtaposing the pictures of when they were happy against the weight of the family's current situation made her tear up. Charles was on the brink of insanity, fighting a never-ending battle. Julia, though possibly a formidable ally, was forever incorporeal, and no longer able to be with her family.

Ramona began to realize the full gravity of the situation. There was not going to be a happy ending for Dex and his family even if they did beat back the creature. What plan were they trying to come up with?

She looked up and saw Dex was watching her. "Hey," he called softly. "I'm ready. Are you?"

She wiped a tear from her cheek and nodded slowly. Mindful that others could hear her, she said, "Uh. Yeah, I guess. As ready as I'm going to get."

Dex had been busy. He had drawn a large circle on the carpet as well as the other symbols. She noticed that he had flipped the blackboard over and had written something on it. She couldn't read what; it was in one of the few languages she didn't recognize.

"Step carefully inside and sit facing me. Remember, once she is with you, talk out loud. I need to hear what she says. Don't worry about what I might think or anything like that. It's important I hear what she wants me to know. Remember, we are trying to come up with a plan, okay?" Dex oddly stressed the last part.

Ramona nodded. "Yes, I get it." After a brief pause, she continued, "Dex, what if this is the last time you ever get a chance to talk with her? Do you want to tell her anything?"

Dex's face was tight and he ground his teeth. "I know, Ramona. I know." He glanced briefly at the blackboard. "Try and focus on two things, driving that creature away and getting out of here alive." His voice was rough with emotion.

Stepping into the circle, she settled down in front of him. Dex began to chant.

Soon, images started flashing. They got stranger as she tensed up in confusion. If Julia was trying to get in, she wasn't having much luck. Ramona briefly wondered if this was going to work before she remembered she had to invite Julia in.

She pictured a room in her mind. She thought of a door and that she was opening this door. Immediately, she felt a weight on her chest, making it harder to breathe.

"Julia?"

"I'm here," Ramona heard her own voice in her ears and felt her mouth moving. *Freaky!*

"Uh, nice to meet you? Um, is it okay that I call you Julia?" Ramona spoke out loud as Dex wanted her to, but it was really freaking her out!

Ramona heard a light laugh in her head that her own throat didn't echo. "Yes, given the situation, you may call me Julia, Ramona."

Still weird to hear her own voice. Ramona knew she was tense and tried to relax. It wasn't easy; her eyes shifted from looking at Dex to the blackboard. Julia was reading what Dex had written, but Ramona still had no idea what it said.

"Julia, Dex read your journal. He knows what you wrote and about the.." Ramona started to say.

"Hush. Do not speak of it. *It does hear all but does not see without a body.*" Julia only 'spoke' the last part in Ramona's head.

Images of filing cabinets flashed in her mind. She saw the drawers being opened and files flying out.

"Hey, stick to the more recent events," Ramona said out loud.

"I am. I have no desire to know my son that well," Julia said, also out loud. Probably more to reassure Dex.

"But you want to know about me, don't you? You are going back before I knew him, aren't you?"

"*Clever,*" Julia said, again, only in her mind.

"And Dex is always telling me to focus!" Ramona grumbled. "*What are you looking for?*" Ramona asked Julia silently.

"About you, generally speaking, *and what you are capable of specifically. And yes,* I also want to know what you know about, Dexter. *You are right, this will be the last time we are together.*" Julia spoke both silently and out loud.

Thoughts were quicker than words, so it wasn't glaringly evident what she was doing, though Ramona suspected Dex knew. He couldn't speak and maintain the incantation at the same time. Being so close to his mother but not being able to speak to her must be like a kind of torture, Ramona thought to herself.

"*Yes,*" Julia said, agreeing with her.

"*I knew if something went wrong, Dexter would eventually read my journal. In it, I said that if I failed in my last incantation the only way to save Philip from the creature would be to sacrifice him to Cthulhu, the Dreamer. Dexter agrees that this must be done.*"

Friggin' hell! Dex must have written that on the blackboard. "*But what about you? And how does that help us?*" Ramona didn't like having a conversation in her own head; there was no way of filtering and *not* saying to Julia what she was thinking.

"*Dexter has suggested that he sacrifice us both. When you came here the first time, Dexter could not draw a lesser creature to our house because, presumably, it feared the creature already here. Dexter is proposing that bringing a Great One forth will cower the creature, forcing it to retreat.*"

"And you are okay with this plan?", Ramona said out loud, looking straight at Dexter.

"*Yes, it is what must be done. I couldn't save my daughter, Anna, but I can save my son. Having been estranged from him for so long, it will bind us together as a family again,*" Julia replied. Dex nodded just once.

"And Charles, we have to save him, too, don't we?" Ramona asked, trying not to cry. Dex shook his head, his eyes red.

Julia was stern, but comforting, "*He will welcome the release. And the gift of power that it will bring his son. Charles will die but he will be fully himself, neither insane nor a slave to that thing.*"

"I get how to sacrifice Charles, but how can you be sacrificed?" Ramona silently thought to Julia

"*It's complicated; the nuances are difficult to explain. Dexter must take his place as head of the family and hold all within the house under his reign. By doing so, he will have power over me, which I will not dispute. All he has to do is find a way to indicate and symbolize his willingness to sacrifice me. The Great Old One will do the rest."*

"What can I do?" Ramona asked both Dex and Julia.

*"Tell Dexter, Charles and I understand. I am willing to give myself to the Dreamer as my father did before me. His father and I know that he loves us and that he is doing what must be done. We respect his courage and that he honors his family. Most of all, tell him we love him."*

Dexter was still chanting softly, as he maintained the incantation, but his eyes were filled with pain. She nodded to him, agreeing to the plan. Her throat was so tight, she had to struggle to say, "I love you." Dex closed his eyes briefly, almost breaking the cadence of his chant by breathing so hard.

*"Thank you, Ramona,"* Julia said. *"You can also tell him that I approve of his relationship with you and that I hope you choose to join our family. Always comfort each other and may you both find peace."*

"Goodbye, Julia," Ramona said, as the tears rolled down her cheeks.

Suddenly, Julia was gone. Ramona fell forward, towards Dex, disorientated and exhausted.

He caught her, holding her close, he whispered, "Thank you."

Without warning, there was a thunderclap of sonic concussion in her head. Crying out in pain, she instinctively ducked.

"That's the creature's mental attack. I expect Mother deflected what she could," Dex told her. "Can you stand? She will be able to hold it off, but not for long. 'We have to get out of here.'"

Ramona could hear the quotes as Dex spoke.

Dex stood up and pulled her to her feet. "C'mon, neophyte, it's time."

# Chapter Thirteen

The house shook again as they both heard Charles pounding on the study door. Dex flipped the chalkboard over to the incantation side and put his hand flat against it, over the center part. He looked at Ramona as he started chanting. She quickly centered herself and began to chant, as well, to add her power to his.

The writing started to glow like empowered warding symbols. With a flash of intuition, she understood Dex had empowered the writing to be a symbol of his mother and her current state of being.

While she droned on, Dex switched to begin chanting the first part of the incantation—opening the way to the void.

The door burst open, as Charles broke through. The presence of the hideous, unseen horror was overpowering.

The thing controlling Charles made him laugh; the sound strange and unnerving. "You can't hurt me! Don't worry, I won't kill you, there is too much to feed on!"

Drawing her knife from her pocket, Ramona flipped it open with a smooth motion. Dex took the knife from her and started the second part of the incantation—invoking Cthulhu.

The creature screamed, "No!" and rushed at them blindly.

Ramona stepped in front of Dex and met Charles with a sharp jab, breaking his nose. As they struggled, Dex got in behind him and slashed his throat.

## Homecoming

Blood pouring from the gash, Charles fell to the ground, as his puppeteer dropped him like a marionette. Dex moved to the blackboard and pulled his bloodied hand down through the incantation; erasing the symbols and essentially breaking the binding that held his mother to her incorporeal form.

Ramona and Dex both felt the power burst out as the energy from the sacrifices was released.

There was no eye to be seen, but Ramona knew Cthulhu was there, taking what had been given to him. The hideous, foul presence waned, as it scurried away from the Great Old One, who was so much more powerful than itself.

Ramona and Dex both dropped to their knees, exhausted and spent. Dex began to cry. Ramona crawled over and put her arms around him, holding him as tight as she could.

## Chapter Fourteen

When he was able, Dex stood up and wiped at his eyes. He shook his head when Ramona tried to speak.

He went over to his mother's desk and opening the middle drawer, took out a small red box. He put it in his backpack and slung it over his shoulder.

Then, he simply turned and walked out.

Nonplussed, Ramona picked up her knife, quickly wiped it and put it away. She took one last look around before grabbing her backpack and hurrying to catch up with Dex.

They climbed into the van and drove off.

Looking down at herself, she saw that she was wet with blood, which was going to get sticky real soon. Gross.

"Are we going back to the cabin?" she asked him.

"Yes, for now."

"Then what?"

He shrugged. "I thought we'd go to Europe. Travel; maybe finish our degrees."

"Okay. I'm guessing money isn't an issue?" she asked.

"Nope."

"Just finish our degrees? We wouldn't be studying anything else?"

"There are people, friends of my grandfather, who might teach us. Make us stronger." Dex looked meaningfully at her.

"We would come back here then?"

## Homecoming

"Eventually. When we are ready."

"It's not over?" she asked him, already knowing the answer.

"No."

"Sounds like we need to make a plan."

# RECKONING

# Reckoning

# Chapter One

Dexter climbed out of his rental car and leaned against it as he looked up at his house.

It had been five years since he had come home to find an unseenable horror loose in his family's house. His father had been on the brink of insanity and his mother, who he had presumed dead, was incorporeal. They were both locked in a continuous battle with the horror.

Dexter had sacrificed them both to Cthulhu. He had gambled that the coming of the Great Old One would be enough to drive the horror back into its 'den.'

Fortunately, he had been correct, and the creature was once again contained. Its 'den' was the relic it was bound to. His mother's journal had told him about the relic. After the sacrifice, Dexter had left the house, and the country, with his college girlfriend, Ramona. She hadn't been back since.

Dexter had returned only several times. Before he left, Dexter had arranged for the house to be closed up and maintained during his absence. It was potentially hazardous for the caretaker, but Dexter had been reasonably certain that as long as the caretaker didn't perform any incantations or rituals, they would be fine.

He hadn't needed to see to his father's burial or interment, as there was no body. The Dreamer had taken it, as was his due. Dexter also had headstones placed in the local cemetery for both of his parents, but he had yet to visit and pay his respects.

He couldn't, not while that thing was still bound inside the relic that was still inside his house. It was unfinished business; an open wound that had not healed. It had taken five years of research, but Dexter was satisfied he knew as much about the relic's history as he needed. More importantly, he knew enough to decide what he was going to do about it.

Dexter reached into the car, grabbed his large backpack, and slung it on to his shoulder. Slamming the car door shut, he walked defiantly up the stairs and into his house.

His courage flagged as he got inside. The enormity of the grand entryway emphasized its emptiness. Even so, it was less disturbing than on previous occasions. The eerie presence of that abomination was no longer evident.

He wandered from room to room, checking on things, as his memories kept him company.

It was closer to ten years since he had felt truly at home in his house. He wasn't present when his parents, along with his sister Anna, had inadvertently released the creature. When it was initially released, the horror killed Anna. His parents then tried to fight it for several years without telling him. During this time, his parents, Charles and Julia, had consequently decided to keep him away. They had sent him, only sixteen, to stay with friends of the family until he was old enough to leave for college.

Now the house, the grounds, the family library of esoteric and occult tomes, were all his; along with the burden of the relic.

Since his parents' death, Dexter had managed the family's finances well enough. Finishing his degree and traveling through Europe had been a necessary expense, though he had learned ways to offset some of the costs.

He hadn't been alone during this time; he had been with Ramona. She fascinated him in college; strong, beautiful, fiercely smart, and great fun to be around. She had broken up with him over what he decided was a misunderstanding on her part. They got back together a year later after a ritual where she had nearly been sacrificed along with her roommate.

She took the revelations of his worship and its practices amazingly well. And as it turned out, she even had an instinct for the mythos. She traveled with him and assisted in his research while she finished her degree and learned more about the mythos. Ramona meant everything to him.

As a result of his research and various studies, Dexter had gained a respectable reputation within the academic community. He was considered a brilliant scholar and was a lecturer at one of the older universities in Scotland. The university's occult library was more impressive than Derleth College's had been, and even exceeded Miskatonic's collection.

More importantly, Dexter learned how to successfully navigate within the community of his fellow practitioners. He was able to promote amiable discussion and even a sharing of knowledge, albeit on a limited basis, amongst those otherwise reluctant to do so. In addition, he learned the art of the 'tit for tat,' as Ramona mischievously called it.

This was important, as money alone wasn't enough to get access to private libraries and personal collections; there had to be a trade of sorts. More of an 'I'll show you my copy of the Necronomicon if you show me yours'. It was a skill Ramona had a knack for and she was willing to teach him. It was a very valuable asset for Dexter during his hunt.

As Dexter continued to roam through his house, he felt as though it was waking up; like *he* was waking up. It felt good; he felt strangely good. He had assumed his house was weak with the loss of his family and their long battle. Yet it didn't feel like it, rather it felt young and strong; revitalized.

More hopeful, Dexter walked with confidence and greater energy. His plan might work after all.

# Chapter Two

Ramona sat in a large, overstuffed chair in the parlor, reflecting on the past five years of her life. She was in the manor house of an old friend of the Phillips family. She was from what the European locals liked to call 'humble' origins. Being in a parlor, in a manor house, still felt odd to her.

The last several years had been the best ones of her life. She had finished her degree and was now a travel nurse, certified in several countries across Europe.

She, like Dex, was a practitioner, and also worshipped the Dreamer. She was not like him in some ways but had never bothered to figure out just what she was exactly. She was more than a neophyte or generic cultist, but certainly not a Priest like Dex. She was a capable practitioner and could perform certain rituals, but she wasn't into that aspect as much as he was.

She enjoyed reading the tomes and handling the relics. Languages had always come easy for her and the ancient languages of some of the books were a thrilling challenge. She had enjoyed studying with Dex when they were undergraduates, which made the time they spent together in research more fun than work. She loved Dex more than she had thought was possible.

Her skills as a researcher were well-respected in the academic and occultist communities, for one so new to practicing. She was a reader at the same university where Dex was a lecturer. Her reputation was further enhanced by the fact that she was well able to handle herself in a fight or when things went other than as expected during a ritual or incantation.

Her combined knowledge of nursing and occult made her much sought after, especially after the rituals or incantations went wrong. It was often a particularly complex endeavor to fix or heal the aftereffects of a failed ritual, as well as its potential hazards. Ramona found herself drawn to the work. She originally studied nursing because she liked helping people, and now she was uniquely qualified to do so.

Still sitting in the comfortable armchair, Ramona mused that now it was all coming to an end. Dex had decided that it was time to confront the entity they had been researching. She, however, wasn't as certain as he was. She remembered a time when she was the one ready for a fight and he had been the one more accepting of the status quo. Now, she had a life she didn't want to lose it.

Conflicted, Ramona wanted to fight like hell to keep what she loved, but at the same time, she didn't want to fight at all. She just wanted to stay safe and keep things the way they were.

Dex had strongly argued that they couldn't move forward until the horror was gone. Ramona suggested that it was *Dex* who couldn't move forward, but he was adamant in his decision to confront it.

He argued that neither the relic, or the events surrounding his family's acquisition of the relic, were something that could just be buried and forgotten about.

He finally convinced her by sharing Julia's and his sister Anna's journals with her. Anna had written in her journal how the Phillips family had been given the relic. Julia's journal confirmed what Anna had written before her death. After reading the journals, Ramona had to admit she felt a burning desire to make things right.

It had been two months since she had agreed to help Dex with his plan. They had been apart, with no contact, for two long months. So much could have happened. What if something had changed? So much could go wrong; it was more likely they would die tonight than they would live.

Ramona was scared and conflicted; she wasn't sure she could go through with the plan.

# Chapter Three

After his making his rounds of the house, Dexter brought in the rest of the supplies from the car. He put his suitcase in the master bedroom and tried not to call it his parent's bedroom. It was his now. He had to remember that. He was the head of the house.

Dexter braced himself before going into his father's study. And it was still his father's study. It was the one room he hadn't asked, Alfred, the caretaker, to pack up; it was just as his father, Charles, had left it five years ago.

The large, heavy wood desk dominated the room. On it sat the relic—an innocuous-looking statue, an ancient Egyptian ushabti, otherwise known as a shabtis. Carved in stone, it was meant to hold the Ka of a pharaoh. Instead, this ushabti held an entity from beyond the void.

Dexter seated himself in the oversized desk chair, remembering his father sitting in it as he did. After a time, he stopped waiting for the uncomfortable feeling to pass and started opening the drawers. He felt like a kid doing something bad; he felt as if he was going to get caught and yelled at, but at the same time, he felt a child's curiosity to see what his father kept in his desk.

After rummaging through the center drawer and the three drawers on the left, he sat back, disappointed. He hadn't found anything out of the ordinary. Soldering on, he searched the drawers on the right side. This time, he found what he was looking for—his father's journal.

As he skimmed through it, Dexter wasn't surprised he couldn't make out the cipher. Curiously though, the page marker was not on the last written page.

Dexter looked closely at the page marked until he found two short sentences his father had written plainly, not in the cipher: "Who in the world am I? Ah, that's the great puzzle."

He recognized it as a quote from Lewis Carroll's "Through the Looking-Glass". Was the quote supposed to be a clue for the cipher?

He thought for a bit before realizing it wasn't the quote itself that was the clue. Dexter pulled open the center drawer and found the small, ornate magnifying glass he had seen earlier. Holding the lens over the page, he found he could read the journal if he read it through the magnifying glass.

Dexter looked more closely at the magnifier. Old-fashioned and elegant, he would never have guessed it was a relic.

Skimming through the journal, he focused on the entries of the last several months. It was difficult to read about his father's struggle with the entity, and Charles's final entry was written directly to him, apparently on the day he died. Tearing up, Dexter swallowed hard. He couldn't read it and keep his composure. It would have to wait; he had a schedule he had to keep.

Closing the journal decisively, he stood up and gathered his courage. Grabbing the ushabti, he took it downstairs. What would have been a billiard room in other houses, was a ritual chamber in his.

Normally, the chamber would have contained an altar, but Dexter had arranged for it to be temporarily removed. He put the ushabti down on a precisely marked spot on the floor.

For this ritual, he wanted the space to be as empty as possible. Other than the relic, the only other items in the room were six incandescent stones arranged in a pattern on the floor.

As he finished preparing the room, he made sure the doors and windows were locked and sealed. He did not want any interruptions. As a last-minute precaution, he added several new warding symbols and refreshed the existing ones.

Dexter had put some thought into how he would dress for this ritual. He wanted items from each member of his family, including his grandfather, to both symbolize family unity and to form an unbroken line of power through the generations of his family.

He pulled on his robe and tied it closed with his father's embroidered sash. On his left arm, he strapped on his mother's wrist gauntlet with her favorite dagger. He slipped his grandfather's signet ring onto the pinkie finger of his left hand. On his right wrist, he wore Anna's elder sign link bracelet. He was already wearing the pendant Ramona had given him around his neck.

Dexter put his hand on the pendant briefly, remembering how insistent she had been that he never take it off. He hoped she still remembered and would be there for him now.

Stepping into the center of the circle, Dexter didn't give himself any more time to doubt. He took a small vial from a pocket of his robe, opened it, and quickly swallowed the contents. He immediately started chanting to open the way into the void.

It didn't take long before he felt the now familiar, eerie presence of the horror. His incantation had partially released it, like his family unknowingly had. This time, he was ready for it. He could feel it nearby, but it was not yet attacking.

Dexter completed the first and second incantations before opening his eyes. He could only see within the small space outlined by the incandescent stones. The relic was still in its spot. Outside the perimeter, all else was black.

He wasn't really expecting to see an unseen able entity, but he wouldn't have been surprised if he had, now that they both were gone from his home and were out in the void itself.

"Hello. I know you can hear me. I would speak with you, if you are willing," Dexter said out loud.

There were no sounds to hear, but Dexter felt the concussion of a heavy hit against one of his wards. Looking down, he saw the ward was weakened but still intact.

"Yes, I will speak with you," a voice said from inside his head.

Dexter decided that the creature had gotten partially through his ward; enough to speak with him, but not enough to get control of him. Nervous, he tried to calm himself. This was the plan after all.

Speaking quickly, he told the creature, "I have a problem that it might suit you to help me to resolve. I am now the sole owner of the relic that binds you. I do not want to keep it, but I cannot give it away without dooming others to my family's fate. If I were to bury it, it does not entirely relieve me of its burden and still leaves you bound."

"Quite a problem. For you. For me, killing the sole owner frees me," the creature answered.

"Not entirely. My research indicates you've done that before. That freed you to propagate death and mayhem, but you were still tied to my realm. And, eventually, the relic was once again claimed, and you subjugated to another's will," Dexter spoke in the tone of an academic addressing a colleague.

"I am more than capable of breaking the will of you fragile creatures."

"That is short-term thinking, unless you want to stay bound in a corporeal realm with us puny creatures."

Dexter felt the creature move within his mind, like a snake slithering through the grass.

"There is an alternative?" the entity asked.

"I believe so," Dexter calmly replied. "I, the sole owner of the relic, would be willing to break the binding that holds you to it and my realm. Here. We are currently outside of my realm. Once that is done, you will be free to exist out in the void."

"Why would you do this?" the entity asked. Dexter felt the creature trying to probe deeper into his thoughts. "And why should I help you, when I can just kill you and continue to have fun torturing you horrible little creatures?"

"Because you don't have time to kill me. I have already swallowed poison that will kill me before you can break me. If I die before you get control, you will remain trapped, not only bound to the relic, but here within this pocket space, out in the void. My death will seal you in, alone, forever."

Dexter felt a sudden pain in his head. He steeled himself and concentrated to counter the attacks of the entity. They struggled, for how long, Dexter couldn't be sure; time could well move differently here, but eventually the creature stopped.

"What do you want from me?" the entity asked.

Breathing hard but determined, Dex answered, "I want a reckoning with those who brought you to my family and you are aptly suited to do what I want done."

# Chapter Four

Ramona checked the time. It was too soon. *Friggin' hell.* She stood up, angry, but still scared. *"I can't leave Dex again; I have to help,"* she thought to herself. *"I am no match for the creature, nor am I a very strong practitioner. I wish I was a wizard, but magic doesn't really exist. The magic we know in this realm is just illusions; tricks of diversion. To help, Dex needs a very good magician."*

She took another tour around the parlor; all the wards were correctly drawn and fully empowered. It had taken days to create them all. There were so many wards and other symbols that the atmosphere in the room was thick with power.

In addition to the wards, she had placed several easily identifiable relics around the room. Some of them were devoid of the power they once held. She hoped that her guests would assume the power in the room came from the relics and not her wards. She had tried to hide many of those.

There was a particularly elegant relic on the table in the center of the room—a magnificent showpiece like no other on the planet.

It was made of a metal not found on earth—bright like polished aluminum, yet stronger than any known element. It was shaped like a sinuous piece of modern art and stood close to four feet high. One might call its coloring silver, but the color writhed and shifted the more someone stared into it.

## Reckoning

Given its value, her guests should not be surprised she had placed protecting wards around it.

Ramona was certain it would draw a significant amount of attention, though conversely, she didn't want her guests to think about it too much. *So many things could go wrong*, her brain reminded her.

The room was lit by electric light. Unlit candles had also been placed around the room; in case they were needed. The more mundane items were also in place. Against the wall, there was a side table with a tray of crystal glasses and two decanters filled with a fine vintage. Nothing was too good for the guests she was expecting.

Ramona checked the time again. She hoped everyone would arrive promptly. Everything had to be in place very soon now.

The doorbell chimed, indicating at least one guest would be early. Leaving the parlor, Ramona went to the front door and peered out the side window.

Driscoll Wescott stood outside, looking around nervously. He seemed unaware she could see him through the simple mechanism of one-way glass. Ramona would have preferred to spend as little time as possible with the over-sized worm, but he was here, and she didn't want to lose him now that he was.

With a wide, gracious smile she opened the door, saying, "Mr. Wescott, how wonderful you were able to come. Please come inside." Ramona spoke in English but deliberately thickened her Spanish accent.

"Ah, gracias, Miss Guerrero. Thank you," Wescott replied, as he stepped into the foyer.

Still smiling pleasantly, Ramona said, "You are the first guest to arrive. Would you please go through to the parlor?"

Wescott, hesitated, "Well, I hope I am not too early. I just like to get the lay of the land, so to speak. I'm sure you understand." He looked at her doubtfully.

Ramona nodded, only giving him a noncommittal 'of course.' She gestured again, indicating the door to the parlor. He still hesitated. Ramona wasn't sure if he hesitated because he thought a lady should precede him, or if he was worried that she would attack him from behind. Either was possible with him. Ramona waited patiently until he gave an awkward cough and went into the parlor.

The doorbell chimed again, sparing Ramona from making small talk with him. "If you will excuse me; please help yourself to some refreshment."

This time, Rowley Whitney was at the door. He stood confidently as he waited, rocking slightly on the balls of his feet. Oh good. She definitely wanted him here.

She opened the door and said, "Good evening." Her tone was somber, and her face was impassive.

Whitney looked her up and down before answering, "Good evening, Miss Guerrero, isn't it? I believe I was invited to the showing?"

"Yes, certainly. Please come in."

Whitney strode past her into the foyer and straight through the open door into the parlor with the arrogance of the entitled. Ramona held her face steady but couldn't control a little eye roll before following him. *Jerk.*

Inside, the two men eyed each other. "Gentlemen, do you not know each other?" Ramona asked. "My apologies. Mr. Rowley Whiney this is Mr. Driscoll Wescott." Turning to Driscoll she said, "Mr. Whitney is from the United States and has a similar interest in antiquities."

Looking at Rowley, she said, "Mr. Wescott is quite the nomad, but currently resides in London. He has an extensive collection of artifacts." She smiled innocently.

# Reckoning

The two men nodded politely to each other but neither said anything. Rowley went straight to the side table and helped himself to a drink.

Ramona was having fun. The ruse was simple. The invitation was to see a powerful relic with the possibility of its purchase. Neither should have assumed it was a private showing. It was fun because Rowley was from an old family of practicing worshippers, though currently well out of favor, and Driscoll was a well-known, if inept, cultist hunter. The two should have at least heard of each other, and it would be reasonable to presume that they also had strong feelings of dislike for each other. *Well, if I'm going to die, at least I'll take these two jerks with me*, she thought to herself.

Driscoll saw Rowley down his drink with no ill effects, so he determined that it must not be poisoned. He allowed Ramona to pour him a drink before taking a seat in one of the chairs.

Rowley, not at all shy, helped himself to another before claiming the other armchair. The atmosphere was decidedly tense.

Fortunately, the lady guest had decided to not be fashionably late. After being let in, she preceded Ramona into the room with a condescending air. Rowley immediately stood and nodded politely.

Driscoll eyed Madame suspiciously. She glared at him until he stood. Ramona, hoping they weren't going to try and claim they didn't know each other, quietly locked the parlor door while she waited for them to finish their little scene before making the final introduction.

"Gentlemen, please allow me to introduce Madame Liliana Grigorescu. Madame Grigorescu has access to the finest collection of 'antiquities' in Paris."

Madame Grigorescu nodded politely to Ramona, who had pronounced her name perfectly. Ramona was not pandering when she praised Madame's collection. However, she was far from a reputable dealer. Grigor, as she was called behind her back, was a relic hunter and was known to be a very cutthroat businesswoman. Ramona knew both men had done business with her in the past.

She politely indicated a chair to Madame before moving to the front of the room to stand before them. She looked down to check the time and was about to speak when she heard Madame clear her throat meaningfully.

When Ramona looked at her, Madame looked between the two men, with their drinks in hand. Ramona bit back a retort and hastily served Madame a drink.

Once again in front of the room, Ramona said, "Thank you all for coming. As you can all see the merchandise, allow me to begin."

Rowley eyed her suspiciously as he had seen her lock the door, but he shrugged, and muttered, 'go ahead.'

Driscoll, ever nervous, said, "Begin what? The bidding, you mean?"

Madame snorted. "She means the incantation. She has to prove it is what she claims it is. To *me*, anyway. *I* don't waste my money on fakes."

"Incantation? For what? Here and now? Shouldn't we stop her?" Driscoll half-rose from his chair.

Rowley growled, "Relax. Sit down and enjoy the ride, Wescott."

Ramona ignoring the side chatter was already chanting; it was time.

She made it through the first chant and opened the void. When she started the second chant, Madame and Rowley exchanged looks. Seeing that, Driscoll again started to protest.

The lights in the room suddenly went out, yet it was still well-illuminated within a certain radius.

"Hey, stop what you are doing!" Driscoll ordered Ramona as he stood up.

Rowley also stood and moved in front of Driscoll, blocking his way to Ramona. "Relax, Driscoll. Nothing is wrong."

Madame slowly got to her feet; her eyes fixed on Ramona. She moved to the sinuous relic and held her hand over it. Ramona shook her head curtly, still chanting.

Though well-experienced practitioners, neither Rowley nor Madame could hear that Ramona had switched to a third chant. When she was done, she nodded to Madame.

Madame flicked the relic, immediately releasing a wave of energy. Each person present felt the energy move through them as they heard the relic begin to 'sing' in a strangely rhythmic cadence.

Six points on the floor suddenly lit up with an incandescent light.

Driscoll, nearly panicked, gaped mutely. Rowley turned to Ramona and said sternly, "Okay. Enough is enough. What is going on here?"

"Relax, Rowley. Ramona was just bringing me to the party," Dexter told him.

# Chapter Five

Everyone turned to stare at Dexter, who now stood opposite from Ramona on the other side of the room.

Madame scowled and muttered something derisive in French. Driscoll tried to draw a gun but was roughly stopped by Rowley.

"Not a good idea to hurt either one of us, if you want to get back," Dexter told them all firmly.

He looked over at Ramona. He didn't say anything, but she could see he was having difficulty breathing.

"The pendant I gave you. Break it open carefully and inject yourself in the neck!" she told him quickly.

They all watched as Dexter immediately grabbed a pendant from around his neck and cupping it carefully in his hands, snapped it open. He took what looked like a small ampule and jabbed himself in the neck.

After a minute, he looked over at Ramona and nodded, smiling in relief.

She smiled back, but only relaxed slightly. There were still so many things that could go wrong.

"I demand to know what is going on here!" shouted Driscoll.

Dexter calmly sat down on the settee. He had waited a long time for this moment, and he was going to take his time.

He felt the entity leave his mind. He was both relieved and worried. Now that it was gone, he didn't want it back, not even part way, but he was worried what it might do to Ramona.

"Gentlemen," Madame called out in a hard voice, "I think I know what this is about." She gestured at the floor near her.

Neither Ramona nor Dex moved, but the two men looked over to see the ushabti relic.

Madame looked daggers at Dexter.

"We've been ambushed!" cried out Rowley.

"It's a dirty trap!" shouted Driscoll.

Dexter returned Madame's look without blinking. He shrugged and said, "Trap or ambush; it doesn't matter now, does it?"

"What do you want from us?" Madame demanded icily.

"For the moment, just to talk. I think I've figured most of it out, but I would like to confirm if you don't mind."

"I also would like for you to explain, if you can, why you chose to do what you did to my family." Dexter's voice had a dead stillness that Ramona had never heard before. Her heart ached for him as her stomach got tight in fear. He sounded like a man ready to die.

"Let's start at the beginning; with the binding of the entity to the ushabti. You may sit down if you like, this may take a while," Dexter told them.

The three did, while Ramona remained standing, ever vigilant. Rowley glanced warily over his shoulder at her. He knew her reputation and wasn't entirely comfortable with her at his back.

"Driscoll, did you know that it was one of your sort that originally bound the entity?" Dexter asked, as if amiably.

"My sort? Whatever do you mean," Driscoll asked cagily.

"Drop the pretense. We all know who you and your fellow do-gooder are. You believe you are a hunter and you run around saving mankind from the scourge of us cultists. For our part, we generally think you are a bunch of idiots who do more harm to yourselves than you do to us."

Glancing around, Driscoll saw Madame nod in agreement. Rowley, shrugged at him, saying, "Yes, it's true. You get lucky occasionally, but for the most part, you are only a nuisance; off chasing your tails most of the time."

"My research has indicated that someone similar to yourself disrupted a ritual, and thinking they were saving the world, bound it 'safely' into the ushabti statue."

"How can you possibly expect me to confirm something that happened several hundred years ago?" Driscoll blustered angrily.

"I can confirm." Those watching saw Driscoll's mouth move, but the voice was different. As his mouth continued to speak, Driscoll's eyes widened in terror. "I was called by a ritual and came to accept the sacrifice that was offered to me. As I was leaving, I felt the binding. Corporeal existence was strange and new to me and I was unable to adapt quickly enough to escape."

Rowley stood up and backed away quickly. Pale and trembling, he said, "It's here? Loose? You brought it with you? It's free?"

Dexter smiled thinly. "Quite a shock, isn't it? To have it suddenly spring out at you like that? Sit down, if you can; we will get to your part soon enough."

Temporarily released, Driscoll stood up, grabbed his gun, and started waving it around, unsure where to point it.

"Point it at yourself, you fool, if you think shooting will help," Madame said with a sneer.

"Idiots. You call me and my brethren idiots, when you brought this creature to our world! It's your fault!" Driscoll was shaking but still felt righteous.

"I disagree," Rowley's mouth began. After a short struggle, the creature left him and returned to Driscoll.

"I was able to watch your puny efforts as I was passed around by your 'brethren.' While none of you horrid creatures understand, your lot understands least."

"The amount of pain and suffering you brought on yourselves by your feeble attempts to master the forces and entities of my realm was highly amusing. It made my imprisonment less torturous."

Ramona wasn't sure if it was losing the fight with the entity or at what it said, but Driscoll suddenly looked desolate.

"What does any of that have to do with me?" he asked feebly.

"Don't you recognize the statue?" Dexter asked him. "You didn't sell it to Madame Grigorescu?"

Plainly terrified and not wanting the entity to answer for him, Driscoll nodded quickly. "Yes, I did sell it to her. But I didn't know that thing was in it! I didn't know!"

"No, but you did steal me from a dead colleague," Madame's mouth told them. Her battle with the entity was very physical. She writhed in her chair and gripped the arms tightly. Despite this, her mouth continued on, "You wanted the money, so you took me without asking the widow whom you had just lain with."

# Chapter Six

"And this brings us to Madame Grigorescu," Dexter said, disgusted, but ignoring Driscoll's despicable immoral behavior for the time being.

Looking at Madame, Dexter continued, "Now, do you claim to be so knowledgeable of the mythos and its relics, and also that you didn't know the ushabti statue contained the entity?" He sounded like he genuinely wanted to know.

Madame continued to writhe; her lips pressed defiantly together. Ramona wasn't sure, but she thought the creature was having fun as it fought with Madame. She didn't know which she preferred, to watch the fight or have the entity go back to a broken Driscoll. He had suffered, but at least they would get an answer and could move on.

Madame suddenly screamed and seemed to pass out. Her eyes rolled back in her head, but the entity continued to use her to speak. "She knew. She didn't want the onus of owning me, so she sold me to the first family she could. She lied to them about the power they felt within the ushabti."

Rowley had been silent, but at the confession, he swore angrily. He stormed over and grabbed Madame's shirt front; shouting down at her as he slapped her repeatedly with his other hand. "You knew! How could you? You brought that thing to my house! It destroyed us!"

Driscoll and Dexter hurried to restrain Rowley. Ramona, though closer, stood quietly still.

Madame's eyes were open and looking at Rowley; blood was coming from her nose and the cut on her lip.

Restrained by the other two men, Rowley spat on her. They dragged him over and shoved him into his chair.

"What else could I do? I couldn't keep it. It would have destroyed me!" Madame told him before looking away from the hate in his eyes.

Dexter looked at Ramona; he couldn't believe what he was hearing. He expected a look of sadness or compassion. Instead, while the others were reacting to the emotional scene, she quickly glanced meaningfully down at her feet then looked over at his. She looked up quickly so no one would notice the exchange.

Perplexed, Dex looked surreptitiously around. There were wards carved on the bare floor. What for? They didn't look like protection symbols, and the area was somewhat small. Just big enough for someone to stand in. Like Ramona was doing. He stood up and moved within the space.

Ramona nodded quickly; her eyes intense. She mouthed 'stay.'

Dexter didn't fully understand her intentions, though he did get that she had her own agenda. Making a brief, 'I'm sorry' face at her, he left the protected area to go pick up the ushabti.

Ramona, her heart beating fast with anticipation, was sick at being denied when they had been so close. She closed her eyes and tried to breath; she could do nothing else now but wait for the time to be right again.

Dexter felt the creature near, as if it were over his shoulder. *I remember my promise to you*, he said in his head. He felt a brief pain as the entity left him; a reminder of its power.

"Rowley Whitney. Yes, your family did suffer the torment of the entity," Dexter said slowly, facing him.

"You were grievously treated and have every reason to be angry at Grigor," he said, turning back to briefly glare at her as he sneered her sobriquet.

Turning back to Rowley, he continued, "What I really want to know though, is after realizing what it was and experiencing what it could do, how do you justify giving the ushabti to my sister, a seventeen-year-old girl?"

Rowley shrank into his chair, knowing he was trapped, but still trying to get away from Dexter, who loomed over him still holding the ushabti.

"I had to. I had to get rid of it. She was old enough to take it on behalf of the family, but too inexperienced to know what it was," Rowley stammered. "It told me to…"

Furious, Dexter swung the statue like a short club, hitting Rowley savagely across his face.

Both Grigor and Driscoll hurriedly got out of their seats and moved across the room, away from Dexter. Driscoll was wildly waving his gun at everyone and no one.

Breathing hard, Dexter stood over Rowley, watching as the blood ran down his face. Rowley himself was unconscious.

He exchanged looks with Ramona. She was extremely tense and breathing almost as hard as he was, but yet still remained within her warding area.

Noting the blood on the end of the ushabti, Dexter turned to face the other two. "I need each of you to give me your blood."

"What? Are you crazy?" shouted Driscoll, pointing his gun at Dexter.

"Never!" Grigor spat definitely.

"They were both previous owners. I need their blood to completely break the binding."

# Reckoning

Grigor immediately understood that Dexter was talking to the entity and began to chant.

Driscoll, only understanding he was in danger, tried to fire his gun at Dex. The entity, not wanting to lose its chance at freedom, entered Driscoll and moved his arm so that the gun pointed at Grigor.

The bullet caught her in the upper chest. She dropped first to her knees, and then fell forward onto her face, dying.

Dexter immediately went and pulled her onto her back, brushing the statue across the wound.

"Quickly, before she dies!" Driscoll's mouth said.

"I know. I know," Dexter muttered. Getting to his feet, he said, "Now I need Driscoll's."

Rowley, coming around, groggily tried to get a grip on the situation.

Driscoll, fighting for his life, shot the gun repeatedly. The entity didn't care where the bullets went as long as none hit Dexter.

Rowley dove for the floor. Rolling to his back, he looked up towards Ramona, assuming she would be coming for him. She wasn't moving, even as a bullet passed through her and hit the wall behind her. Rowley swore, starting to get her ruse.

When the gun was empty, Dexter went over to Driscoll, who the entity was holding still, and drew his mother's knife.

He slashed Driscoll's throat, remembering how he had done the same for his father. The blood poured out and onto the statue. The entity left Driscoll, who dropped to the floor, bleeding out.

Backing up, Dexter moved towards the protected area Ramona had wanted him in earlier, chanting the incantation that would release the entity.

Rowley, screaming, got to his feet and rushed at Dexter. The entity entered into him and the two fought, giving Dexter time to complete the incantation and smash the statue into the floor.

The released energy blasted out, almost taking Dex off his feet. He fell back, stumbling his way into the protected area.

"You fool! You idiot!" screamed Rowley. "Why would you do that? We are all going to die!"

Dex stood still, refusing to answer. In the ensuing silence, the two men heard the low drone of chanting.

Ramona was chanting, activating the wards around Dexter. The entity left Rowley and slammed into the wards. They shook at the force of the hit, but held, unbroken.

"Ramona! No! Save yourself!" Dex shouted to her, certain the creature would go for her next.

"Oh, *she's* okay," growled Rowley. "*She* isn't here." Turning to face her, he continued, "Are you, you little witch?"

The wards fully activated, Ramona stopped chanting and smiled a wicked little smile.

# Chapter Seven

"Magician actually, thank you very much. And, yes and no," answered Ramona. "I am here; just not in body."

"So, what's next? You got Wescott and Grigor. How about me? Neither of you can hurt me. You have no physical presence and he can't leave his little area," Rowley sneered at Ramona. "With that thing free, neither he nor I can open a portal; if it's even possible to open a portal in the void. You aren't in danger, but your boyfriend is. He can't stay in there forever."

Dexter, breathing hard, disorientated from exertion and emotion, wondered the same thing.

"Dex, remind me what your plan was, please?" Ramona asked him, quite calm.

"Well, in order to be free of the relic, I had to break the binding. I could only do that outside of our realm, if I didn't want anyone else to suffer like we did." Dexter, getting himself together, tried to sound like his usual academic self.

"Going out into the void would end things, but if I was going to die, I wanted to die with those who betrayed me and my family."

"You and I came up with a plan. We each would open a way into the void at precisely the same time. The marking stones were all cut from the same relic and have the same resonance. We used them to sync up and join us together."

"I would come with the entity and you would gather the three betrayers together on the pretense of selling them some relic or other."

"I wasn't sure we could get to that point. Once we did, I kept my word and freed the entity."

"Why? Why free it once you had it out here, especially if you thought you were going to die?" asked Rowley. Tired and bloody, he sat in the chair previously occupied by Grigor.

"For two reasons. I did not want it in any way tied to our realm and because I promised I would."

Rowley gaped at Dexter in disbelief. "It killed your sister and destroyed your family and you still kept your word with it? Are you insane?"

"Yes, I kept my word. It is our way. We call out across the void, praying to them, asking for their power. What is lunacy is putting our morals onto what we cannot understand," Dexter replied.

Rowley shook his head. "Yeah, okay. Agree to disagree there. Last question. I understand you were ready to die, but you brought your girlfriend along. What is she to you, your Chosen? Is that how you plan to get out of here, by sacrificing her?"

"That is more than one question, but no. I didn't. I don't have a plan to get out of here. Ramona chose to come. She said she would handle the exit plan. I couldn't know what it was in case the entity got control of me."

Both men looked at Ramona, still standing quietly in her place. Dex thought she looked exhausted, but despite that, he had never seen her looking stronger or more confident.

"You are correct in your suspicion that Dex cannot open a portal from within the void, Mr. Whitney," Ramona said, gravely.

Looking to Dex, she continued, "Some relic or other? Really? I know you had other things on your mind, but you are in the presence of the lost relic of Thoulkesh. It is said to be formed out of metals from Yuggoth."

In awe, Dexter looked at the relic. It was tall, almost shining with luminescence; how could he have been so blind to it all this time?

"How did you ever get a hold of something that utterly magnificent?" Dex asked her. Now that he saw it, he could barely look away.

"Long story for another day," she answered curtly. "But you see how easily I was able to get them here. And because its true nature can only be seen in another realm, they *expected* me to open a portal. They wouldn't have stood by and let me do that under any other circumstance I can think of. The relic of Thoulkesh was both a ruse and a diversion."

Looking fixedly at Rowley she continued, "What Dex told you was partially correct, about how we all got here. We did simultaneously open gateways and the stones did form a connection between us, however, they alone could not have created a stable 'room', like the one we are in now, out here in the void. This room is a result of my intricate set of wards, anchored by some of the other relics."

Ramona, staring at Rowley, was being unusually loquacious. Dex wondered what she was up to. He tried to think, but it was difficult. He was tired, almost devoid of will. After years of effort, he had avenged his family. He was free. He had never thought much past this point.

The low thrum of Thoulkesh was mesmerizing. He was surprised they couldn't hear it.

Ramona continued to speak, still looking at Rowley. "I created this room. I said it was stable, but it's fragile. It wouldn't take much to break it; essentially, I just end my ritual and return my mind to my body."

"The entity should be fine; it would be truly free once more. Of course, that would leave you in a bad way, Rowley, but after what you did to Anna, I'm okay with that."

Dex was getting peeved. Why was she talking to Rowley and not him? This could be the last time they ever saw each other. Okay, it was her turn to twist the knife, so to speak, on Whitney, but what about him?

As he got angry, the thrum increased in intensity.

*Wait a minute!* His tired brain finally caught on to her plan. Before they parted two months ago, she had told him about Thoulkesh and what it was said it could do. He thought then that the exposition of the relic had been interesting; he hadn't realized she had been prepping him.

Looking more closely, he saw there were runes on the table surrounding Thoulkesh. Of course, Thoulkesh had to be protected so that the others couldn't get to it. However, now that he was looking, he saw they were the same as the runes that encircled him, too. They all glowed with the same soft light of power. Did that mean something? The wards around Thoulkesh were to keep others out, as was his. Could it mean that both Thoulkesh and he were within the same protected space, so to speak? They were not physically together, but they were in the void, outside normal space, and maybe the same laws and rules did not apply.

Rowley was making a rude gesture at Ramona, saying, "I don't really care what you think of me. I did what I had to do for my house. And I don't believe you are going to leave your boyfriend in a lurch. So, quit monologuing and let's get out of here."

Dex looked over at Ramona and caught her eye. He crossed his arms and shifted his stance so that he was directly facing Thoulkesh. As he started to chant, she relaxed and nodded at him almost imperceptibly.

## Reckoning

Relief flooded Ramona; Dex had gotten it at last. He realized the protecting wards around him were the same as those around the gateway relic, and that the two were connected. It had been such a gamble. If he hadn't gotten it, she didn't know of any other way she could have sent him home. She forced herself to remain calm; she still needed to distract Rowley.

Schooling her face, she said, "Mr. Whitney, you need to understand what is going to happen. I am going to leave now. Very soon this 'room' will no longer exist. I don't understand the void; maybe you will die or maybe you will float around for a while and be a snack for the entity. I don't know; I don't care."

Rowley scoffed and turned to Dexter on the other side of the room. Dex was no longer there. The Thoulkesh was gone, too.

Panic rising, he looked back to Ramona.

She was gone.

The room started to fall away as he felt the creature wrap itself around his mind, holding it tightly, saying. *"You are my relic now."*

# Chapter Eight

Dexter found himself back in his house. The sudden shift from the non-space of the void back into 'real' space was incredibly disorienting. His equilibrium shot; he fell off his feet onto the floor. Nausea immediately followed, causing him to throw up.

After a time, Dexter was able to get control of himself and stop the now dry retching. Rolling onto his back, away from his puke, he could only lay there, breathing hard, and hope the disorientation would pass.

When it didn't, he forced himself to sit up. He was alone in a locked room. If he didn't help himself, no one would. Ramona, if she made it back, was at least an ocean away.

He half-crawled, half-stumbled his way to the door and opened it. The pressure in his head immediately lessened and it was easier to breathe. Grateful for any respite, he hung onto the door for balance, still trying to get himself together.

He reasoned that he had created a small pocket of protected space within heavily empowered wards that had been joined with or moved to the void. By opening the door, he broke his wards which released any remaining power and allowed for the room to fully integrated itself back into 'normal' space. If this was the case, he should be okay soon enough.

# Reckoning

He slid to the floor and leaned back against the door. He pulled at his robes until he could get his hand into his pocket and take out his phone. He was surprised to see that it was over a week after the day he left. His already upset stomach clenched in fear at what could have happened. Dexter told himself it was only a week; it could have been a lot worse. Hearing a noise, he looked up to see Alfred, his caretaker and personal assistant, rushing towards him.

---------------------

Dexter sat in his study at his desk, nervously trying to read. He was expecting Ramona any time now. They had been in contact by phone over the last couple of weeks. Being so out of it, she had had more contact with Alfred than himself. He wanted that to change as soon as possible. He was fully recovered, and he missed her. He wondered for the hundredth time what she had been doing. She wouldn't tell him any details; she just said she was taking care of some very important things that had to be done as soon as possible. If she was trying not to worry him by being so cagy, it hadn't worked.

Tossing his book aside, Dex stood up and walked out of his study and down the stairs. He thought a walk around the grounds might help settle him.

Stepping out onto the porch, he was surprised to see Ramona in the driveway, just looking up at the house. He ran down the steps and pulled her against him, holding her tightly. She hugged him back, just as tightly.

When he heard her sniffle, he looked down and was surprised to see that she was crying but trying not to. "Hey, it's okay. Everything is all right now. You are safe; I'm okay. You are home now; everything is okay."

160

For some reason, that only made her cry more. He gently guided her over and sat down with her on the steps until the worst had passed.

Wiping her eyes, she sat up and tried to speak. Wanting to help her out, he asked, "Is everything okay? Did you see something wrong with the house?"

Ramona shook her head. "No, in fact, it looks beautiful. Really, really beautiful."

"So, what's wrong?"

With an incredulous look, she replied, "Really? It's been years since I've been back. This is the first time I've seen your house. You know, since the first time I saw it."

Dex just said "Okay, yeah," and waited for her to go on. He felt there was more.

"I also wasn't sure if I should ring the doorbell or just go in."

"Oh. Yeah. I can see how you might think things would be different now. And they are, now that the ushabti is gone. We do need to talk." Dex got to his feet and held out his hand, saying, "C'mon. Please come inside."

Ramona sniffed and wiped her eyes decisively before getting to her feet. "Did you mean what you said about this being my home?"

"Yes."

Dexter turned and walked into the house. Ramona followed him inside. He turned to her, intending to ask if she wanted to talk first or be shown around the house first. She stepped in close, giving him a passionate kiss. The full tour could wait.

---------------------

# Reckoning

Later that afternoon, Dexter and Ramona lay together in what Dexter hoped was their bedroom. "Can we talk about the last couple of weeks now?" he asked her.

"Sure," she answered. "Just the last couple of weeks?" She was playing innocent, teasing him.

Letting her go, he sat up to glare at her, "No, of course not. I mean your exit plan, too. How the hell did you get the Thoulkesh?"

Ramona stretched and sat up. "That took a hell lot of planning and a great deal of effort. I think planning the Normandy invasion was less complex. Essentially, I got it through a series of little favors and trades. I couldn't be blatant about what my end goal was, which made it even more difficult, but eventually, I got it. I was in debt to a great many people, not in money but in terms of a boatload of promises and favors."

"Ramona…." Dex began, seriously worried.

"It's okay," she hastily assured him. "It actually all worked out."

"How?!"

"Madame Grigorescu. Well, her stash of relics actually."

"Ramona! You didn't!!"

"Yes, I did. 'To the victor goes the spoils' or whatever the quote is. It wasn't a big a risk as you think. I convinced her people that she was dead and that I was the rightful owner. It didn't take much negotiating to buy them onto my side. Her people were smart enough to know they didn't want to mess directly with most of her merchandise."

"I spent most of the last couple of weeks figuring out the best way to pay off my debt with her *warehouse* of items."

She nodded at him in answer to his surprise at her choice of word. "Yes, warehouse. I could hardly believe it myself. I had to go through and get rid of the fake stuff, of course. One of the guys wanted it, so he could start his own business, but I said no. I wasn't going to be a party to any sort of scam. I made sure it all got destroyed."

"Of course, the biggest thing was making sure Thoulkesh got 'home' safely. Which reminds me, thank you for letting Alfred pack it up and ship it to me. Its owner is someone we do *not* want to be on the wrong side of."

"You bartered to *borrow* the Thoulkesh?" Dex asked incredulously.

"Yes, essentially," Ramona said with a wicked grin. "I argued it was like having a bank load of money that wasn't working for you. What is the point of having something like that if you never use it or leverage it on your behalf in some way?"

Dex was silent for a time as he tried to take it all in. Finally, he said, "So, you have what is left of a warehouse of relics, books, and tomes?"

"No," she answered sighing. "Between settling my debt, paying off Grigor's people, and getting rid of the fake stuff, was very little of value left. I sold the small stuff for cash to pay off what financial expenses were incurred."

"What matters is that you are debt-free. Right? You are free of any sort of obligation, financial or otherwise?" Dex asked her.

"Yes. I made sure of that. I'm broke, but I owe nothing to no one." Pausing briefly, she went on, "Except for you."

"Don't talk like that. Please. If anything, I owe you more than I could ever repay. Can we please not go there? I didn't think we had that sort of relationship."

"We don't. I just wanted to make sure," she answered, sounding uncertain.

Abruptly changing the subject, she asked, "So, are you okay now? Alfred and I were very worried about you. I was scared you would end up on Yuggoth or not come back for years. It was all such a gamble."

"Yes, I'm okay. I lost a week of time and reacclimating wasn't easy, but I managed. You didn't have to reacclimate at all?" Dex asked, sounding irked.

"No, I wasn't there. Well, not in the corporeal sense. After I got back to my body, it felt like it had all been a dream, but at least I could remember everything."

"I've been trying to put the past behind me. I finally visited their graves and read my father's journal. He left a good-bye note for me, you know," Dex told her sadly.

"No, I didn't know," she answered softly. "Are you okay?"

"I guess. He did know what I was going to do, and he wanted it. He said to tell you he was sorry he tried to kill you and hoped you could forgive him."

Ramona just nodded as she teared up.

"Don't cry. Please. If you do, I will, and I don't want to. I want to move on. I'm ready to look forward."

Ramona smiled, breathing hard with relief. "Okay! So, what do we do now?"

"Well, I could use your help in getting the house together. It could probably use some redecorating. And we need more staff. Alfred cannot manage by himself any longer."

"I guess I could help you. As what? Your girlfriend?"

"My wife, if you will have me."

"Yes!"

# THE CALLING

# The Calling

Day was ending, its light fading across the moor. Whereas daylight shines light into shadowy crevices and chases away the creatures that hide within, here and now, the darkness was stronger than the dying light.

Four figures walked quietly through the gathering darkness. A man in fine robes led the way. A young woman followed behind him; her hands bound by rope in front of her. Two other men carrying large packs followed behind.

"This is it. Stop here", the man in robes suddenly ordered.

The two servants immediately stopped and unshouldered their packs.

Belevis, High Priest of the Great Old One, walked around a large flat stone outcropping, chanting. After the third circuit, he stopped chanting and moved to stand in the center of the stone. He had successfully claimed the site as his.

Scanning the moor, he saw nothing, however, he knew better than to trust his eyes. He was both too old and too wise to be caught in such a way.

Belevis reached his arms up to feel the waning power of the light and wind. He brought his arms down and reached out, palms down to feel the rising power of the earth. He gathered it in, pulling it close to him before suddenly thrusting it away, casting it wide across the moor.

# The Calling

There was an eerie tingle on the back of his neck as he felt the power fall on the creatures already gathered in shadows. He sensed their anticipation as they waited for the night's fall to be complete.

Belevis turned his head away, pretending he hadn't felt her presence out in the dark. Kagath was here.

Some called Kagath, the Child of the Dreamer, or the Chosen. Others said she was the Chosen of the Dreamer. Belevis knew her by reputation only; a priestess who was said to be ancient and learned in the ways of the Great Old One.

Whatever her name, she was here and had to be dealt with. Only he would honor Cthulhu this night. She might have been powerful once, but everything must fall under the weight of time, he told himself.

Belevis directed his servants to ready the ritual site. The altar was not an elevated slab of carved granite. To the untrained, it appeared as an innocuous stone outcropping that the wind and rain had randomly brought forth.

He knew better. The large flat stone had been pushed to the surface by the earth, or rather by He who controls the earth. Cthulhu was restless. The stars alignment told those learned in the ways that He would soon awaken.

Belevis watched as his two underlings laid out his relics and other items upon the altar. His relics, his objects of power, helped anchor the altar to him, and if necessary, could be used as weapons.

When they were done, he encircled the altar with symbols of warding.

The sacrifice watched silently, standing on the altar within his circle. Her dress was thin and too small for her body; it barely covered her, but she did not shiver with cold or fear. He was pleased with his control over her. His domination of her mind made her docile. A weeping, sniveling sacrifice was so tiresome.

Finished with their preparations, the servants took positions on opposite sides, outside of the circle, and knelt down to begin chanting. They chanted in a low, droning tone that resonated with the darkness.

A large, grotesque creature limped its way out of the darkness, into the feeble light of the candles on the altar. It might have been human once, but now its body was so bent and misshapen it was difficult to be sure.

Close now, Belevis could smell its foulness. It had the musty odor of dry decay, but also that of burned flesh. Its skin was as wrinkled as it was scarred.

"Stop. Come no nearer. You may not stand on the altar; I have claimed it for tonight," he commanded.

"Belevis, Bane of Kings, I would speak with you," the hideous creature rasped. "I ask for a parlay; we do not have to be at odds."

"Kagath, Child of the Dreamer. We meet at last. I am sure my reputation precedes me, as yours does you." He was careful not to look the creature in her eyes.

Kagath made a strange sound that might have been a snort of contempt if it came from a human head.

"We are not the only two priests who saw the stars. We should join forces, you and I." As she spoke, she oddly eyed his sacrifice. The girl whimpered and bowed her head submissively.

"I sense no priests, other than you, deceiver."

"My wards are strong; I do not need you to keep the eldritch creatures at bay," he sneered, rejecting her offer of alliance.

"You are a young, arrogant, vain fool. You will not survive the night," Kagath spat at him.

He waved his hand in front of his face, grimacing as the smell of her breath reached him. His wards didn't keep her awful stench out.

## The Calling

"I may not be as old as you, foul-smelling harridan, but I am well-learned in the ways."

"Are you?", she scoffed. "The way you decorate the altar is juvenile. Your robes are heavy and do not permit easy movement; they serve no purpose other than to bring attention to yourself. Who is going to see and care for your meticulously groomed countenance tonight? You look more like a child's doll than a High Priest!"

"Are you calling me vain?" he asked incredulously. "It is not vanity to take care of the body I intend to keep for several more centuries. You would have done well to see to your form, instead of letting it wither and decay as it has."

Kagath sneered contemptuously at him. "Fool," she repeated. "My body is well taken care of and more fit than yours for battle."

Distrustful, but curious, he looked at her more closely. What he had first taken for scars, where actually tattoos etched into her skin. He had heard of these symbols. They were marks of her victories, and they contained power; power that she could draw on at will. He preferred his relics. They too contained power, and he did not have to resort to self-mutilation to access it. He did a quick tally of his relics; from what he could see, he had more relics than she had tattoos.

She looked from his relics to him, and said, "At least I know how to properly choose and bind a sacrifice. That one will hardly please the Great Old One."

Stung by her insult, he failed to grasp her implication. "She will serve," he snapped.

"You will be a better one," Kagath hissed and flung herself into the warding barrier encircling his altar.

Caught by surprise at the sudden attack, Belevis struggled to maintain his wards. Her stench was overpowering; it was difficult to draw breath.

He schooled his mind to focus his will, yet he was furious that such a simple attack might work. She hung in mid-air, suspended by the barrier, screeching and writhing as she fought to break through.

Belevis reached down and grabbed a relic. She was vulnerable to attack, but he had to act now.

With a deafening howl, Kagath broke through and fell to the ground.

Belevis dropped to his knees, stunned with fear and winded from the brief, but intense battle. As he watched her stand, he frantically tried to gather his will to make use of the relic in his hand.

The creatures watching from the dark wailed gleefully at their contest.

Kagath's eyes blazed and fixed on his, as she slowly drew her blade. She started chanting a prayer of offering.

Transfixed by her gaze and unable to draw breath, Belevis knew this was his end. He readied the relic; he would not go alone.

The sacrifice made a sudden movement and smashed a heavy relic statuette into Kagath's head. One hit stunned her, two more dropped her down, bleeding and unconscious.

When had the girl picked that up? How? And how had she used it with enough strength to break it?

No time for that now. Pulling himself together, Belevis got to his feet and faced his sacrifice. "Drop the relic, girl," he commanded imperiously.

The girl looked at him strangely but did not obey.

Too late, he heard the sound of chanting from outside the circle. The relic in his hand shattered and flames burst out, igniting his robes.

The fire spread quickly, forcing him to chant the prayer to dismiss it. He was no neophyte; he could still defend himself, even while chanting.

# The Calling

The girl did not attack. With a quick, ruthless motion, she pulled her hand free from the ropes that bound her before turning away from him to stare out into the darkness.

Belevis turned to see what she was looking at and saw a large, skeletal Hound walk haughtily towards the altar.

He could only watch while the Hound and the girl locked eyes. He felt the wind of the two souls passing each other, as they each returned to their own body.

The fire out, he focused on the woman in front of him. Livid with fury, he commanded, "Drop my relic!"

She smiled sweetly, mutely refusing to obey. As they fought mentally for dominance, he could feel her power; she was no mere girl, but it would not be enough. Not tonight.

The Hound suddenly barked. Belevis felt the sting as the creature's elongated tongue whipped his face. Distracted, he briefly glanced its way.

Chanting the prayer of offering, the girl, Jotral, the rival priest sensed by Kagath, sliced his throat with the sharp edge of his broken relic.

Jotral pushed Belevis to the ground, so his blood would flow out over the altar stone. Once she felt the offering had been accepted, she stopped chanting.

Stepping over the old fool's body, she picked up Kagath's blade. It was simple looking, yet elegant. She would keep this trophy.

She started chanting again, this time to offer the Dreamer his Chosen Sacrifice. Jotral pulled Kagath's head up by her hair and quickly sliced her throat with a single, deft motion.

Once the offerings had been fully accepted, she felt the marks of power manifest on her body. It was less painful than expected; more like a burning so hot that it felt cold. After listening to Belevis and Kagath argue, she decided they both had a point. There was value in keeping your body trim, but it was wise to keep your weapons close in hand.

Exhausted from the ritual, but more so from the preparations she had taken before it, Jotral sat slumped on the cold stone. Her hand and wrist were bleeding from being pulled through the ropes by the Hound when he had inhabited her body.

One of Belevis's underlings suddenly ran at her brandishing a large stick, evidently trying to avenge his master's death.

Fool.

Not for his timing; she was somewhat vulnerable right now, spent and drained as she was.

No, it was more that he underestimated her. Must be the overly revealing dress.

As he reached her, he raised his improvised weapon and looked her in her eyes.

She did not need to engage him in a mental battle of dominance; he was stunned by the force of her will, and the weight of her power crushed his mind.

She looked up and nodded at the Hound. From where he was, the Hound's tongue whipped out and impaled the underling. He was bled dry in moments. When he was done, the Hound approached and sat down next to her, on her left.

She looked right, to the remaining servant.

He immediately bowed obsequiously, saying, "I am your servant, High Priestess."

# ABOUT THE AUTHOR

Stephanie Stieglitz was born and raised in Dover, New Jersey. She graduated Rutgers University with a degree in Comparative Literature. *The Ground Upon Which I Stand* is her one and only trip into Lovecraft's eldritch world. A world where karma can be in the form of a tentacle.

www.ingramcontent.com/pod-product-compliance
Lightning Source LLC
Chambersburg PA
CBHW030330020726
47493CB00004B/1226